Do you like stories that are fun & flirty?

Then you'll ♥ Harlequin® Romance's miniseries—
where love and laughter are guaranteed!

If you love romantic comedies, look for

The Fun Factor

Warm & witty stories of falling in love

**Look out for the next book in the
Fun Factor series...coming soon:**

Mr. Right There All Along
by Jackie Braun in August 2011

Swept Off Her Stilettos
by Fiona Harper in September 2011

Praise for
Nicola Marsh

"What I especially loved about this story was how Marsh was able to take some well-worn tropes and make them seem fresh and lively."
—*The Good, The Bad and the Unread Reviews*
on *Three Times a Bridesmaid...*

"Sterling characters, an exotic setting and crackling sexual tension make for a great read."
—*RT Book Reviews* on
A Trip with the Tycoon

"*A Trip with the Tycoon* is a wonderfully evocative, highly poignant and thoroughly mesmerizing romantic read, which I found absolutely impossible to put down."
—*CataRomance Reviews* on
A Trip with the Tycoon

"Tender, emotional and true to life, poignant romance does not get any better than this!"
—*CataRomance Reviews* on
The Billionaire's Baby

NICOLA MARSH

Girl in a Vintage Dress

The Fun Factor

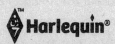

Harlequin®

TORONTO NEW YORK LONDON
AMSTERDAM PARIS SYDNEY HAMBURG
STOCKHOLM ATHENS TOKYO MILAN MADRID
PRAGUE WARSAW BUDAPEST AUCKLAND

Recycling programs
for this product may
not exist in your area.

ISBN-13: 978-0-373-17742-4

GIRL IN A VINTAGE DRESS

First North American Publication 2011

Copyright © 2011 by Nicola Marsh

Nicola Marsh has always had a passion for writing and reading. As a youngster she devoured books when she should have been sleeping, and later kept a diary whose content could be an epic in itself! These days, when she's not enjoying life with her husband and son in her home city of Melbourne, she's at her computer doing her dream job: creating the romances she loves. Visit Nicola's website at www.nicolamarsh.com for the latest news of her books.

For my sister-in-law Deb, the queen of retro chic.
Here's to a future of fabulous frocks,
snazzy shoes and catch-ups over coffee.

CHAPTER ONE

THE moment Chase Etheridge turned into Errol Street the fine hairs on the back of his neck snapped to attention.

Bad enough driving through North Melbourne, the suburb he'd once called home, but this particular street held more than long suppressed memories.

Errol Street encapsulated everything he'd run from, everything he'd rather forget.

Yet here he was edging through traffic, searching for a parking spot, trying to concentrate on the road and obliterate the memories running through his mind like a rerun of a B grade movie.

Riding his bike down to Arden Street to watch his beloved Kangaroos footy team train, walking to the local primary school, picking up Cari from a friend's: not bad memories so much as snapshots of his past. A past where he'd raised Cari and taken on far too much responsibility from a young age. A past filled with making school lunches, correcting homework and cooking dinners. A past where he hadn't had a chance to be a kid.

Though some good had come out of it. Cari adored him and the feeling was mutual. He'd do anything for his sister, the sole reason he was here.

Easing his Jag into a prime parking space, he ignored the uncharacteristic twist of nerves in his gut. Him, nervous? Laughable, as any of his employees at Dazzle would attest to.

Make millions? Take the entertainment industry by storm? Be the best in the business? Could do it with his eyes closed. He didn't have time to be nervous yet striding up a rejuvenated Errol Street, packed with trendy cafés and boutiques and far removed from the street he remembered, he couldn't help but feel a touch anxious.

If being back here wasn't bad enough, strolling into some fancy schmancy vintage shop with the aim of organising his sister's hen's night was enough to send a shiver of dread through the hardest of men.

His mobile beeped and he answered a text message from his PA, one eye on his smartphone, the other on the shopfronts until he spotted his destination.

Go Retro.

Written in candy cane pink in a curly font against a backdrop of shoes and hats and lipsticks, he'd rather be anywhere else but he had business to conduct and that was one thing he did well.

Firing off another message to Jerrie, he nudged the door open with his butt and entered the shop, mentally calculating profit margins and new dates in response to his uber efficient PA's next question.

A tiny bell tinkled overhead but he didn't look up, frowning as Jerrie emailed him the updated guest list for tonight's modelling agency launch.

'Excuse me.'

He held up a finger, not ready to be interrupted while dealing with this latest problem.

'We don't allow mobile phones in here.'

He should've known. A shop dealing in retro stuff would live in the Dark Ages.

'Just give me a minute—'

'Sorry, Retro rules.'

Before he could argue the phone was plucked out of his hands and he finally glanced up, ready to blast the cheeky shop assistant.

'How dare you…'

The rest of his rebuttal died on his lips as his angry glare clashed with the biggest, softest brown eyes he'd ever seen, fringed in illegally long eyelashes that added to an air of fragility.

Not many people stood up to him let alone a five foot six curvaceous blonde who looked as if she'd stepped out of the fifties with her hair pinned up in curls and held back by a headband the same polka dot material as her rock and roll dress.

'I dare because I'm the owner, and rules are rules.'

She pocketed his smartphone, hiding it in the side pocket of a voluminous skirt and having the audacity to smile.

'You'll get it back when you leave. Now, is there anything I can help you with?'

Frowning, he was on the verge of demanding his phone back and marching right back out of here, Cari's hen's night or not, when he caught a glimmer of fear behind those lashings of mascara.

For all her boldness in playing enforcer, the owner of all this frippery didn't like playing the big, bad boss. Something he could identify with so he settled for thrusting his hands into his pockets and glancing around, seeing the place for the first time.

Riotous colour assaulted his senses: fake pink roses stuck on black pillbox hats, orange and teal gloves spilling out of floral boxes, emerald feather boas draped over satin clad mannequins and primrose paisley scarves only a small sampling of the merchandise cramming every nook and cranny of the store.

To his discerning eye, which much preferred sleek modern lines in everything from furniture to fashion, this place was his worst nightmare.

'Can I help you with something specific? An item of clothing? Accessories? A special something for your wife?'

'I don't have a partner,' he said, a blinder of a headache building behind his eyes as he stared at the incredible visual assault of florals and flounces and feathers, glitter and gowns and gaudy baubles that twinkled beneath the muted down-lights, the only concession to the twenty-first century in the entire place.

'Oh. Right. Well, we cater to all types,' she said, a hint of amusement in her low tone as she sized him up and he puffed up in indignation.

'I'm not here for *me*.'

'Nothing to be ashamed of. You're welcome to try on anything you fancy.'

He gaped before snapping his jaw shut. He'd been mistaken for many things in his lifetime; a cross dresser wasn't one of them.

'Are you always this forward with your customers?'

'Only the recalcitrant ones.'

Her encouraging smile lit up her face, adding a spar-kle to her eyes and transforming her from simply pretty to beautiful.

'Well, I hate to burst your sales pitch bubble but the women I date don't doubt my masculinity so I'd appreci-ate it if you did the same.'

She blushed, her smile fading as she looked away, but not before he'd seen that same flicker of vulnerability he'd glimpsed before.

The women he knew, professionally, socially, never showed vulnerability. They were confident: in their tal-ents, in themselves, women who knew what they wanted and weren't afraid to go out and grab it with both hands. This woman was as far from those women as he was from his past yet there was something about her that intrigued him on an intrinsic level.

He'd always trusted his gut instincts and right now, they were telling him to find out what made her tick before he hired her.

She cleared her throat. 'Right, now that we've estab-lished you're not in the market for a nineteen-twenties tangerine tea gown, what can I help you with?'

The corners of his mouth twitched as she continued to eye him dubiously, as if she still wasn't convinced he wouldn't slip into a tulle petticoat when she wasn't looking.

'I heard you did birthday parties.'

She nodded, the huge curl pinned over her forehead wobbling.

'That's right. We can do make-overs, photos, dress ups, the works. Women love it.'

She paused, her lush red-slicked lips curving into a coy smile.

'Some men too.'

He found himself smiling back, when in fact he wanted to say, *Enough with doubting my masculinity already.*

'Would that sort of thing transfer across to a hen's night?'

Her eyes lit up. 'Of course. A few hours of fun for the bride-to-be—'

'I was thinking more along the lines of a week.'

One perfectly plucked eyebrow arched. 'A week?'

'That's right.'

He strolled around the shop, picking up a sparkly hair clip here, a spotted scarf there, not seeing the attraction personally but knowing Cari would adore everything about this place.

And what Cari wanted he'd provide. She was the only person who'd stuck by him all these years and if it hadn't been for her when he was growing up… He suppressed a shudder.

'Let me get this straight. You want me to run a week long hen's party?'

'Uh-huh.'

He stopped at the counter, covered in baskets of womanly paraphernalia and brochures, staggered by the amount of *stuff* draped over every available surface.

'That's impossible.'

'Nothing's impossible,' he said, watching her fiddle with a mannequin, adjusting the wide belt, smoothing the skirt. 'I checked the charges on your website.

I'm willing to double your hourly rate and pay for all transport costs.'

Her eyes widened and, already knowing his offer was too good to refuse, he continued. 'And as CEO of Dazzle, who I'm sure you've heard of, I'm willing to personally recommend you for upcoming events needing something fresh in the way of fashion.'

She stared at him with those big brown eyes, an unwavering stare that made him strangely uncomfortable.

When she didn't jump at his offer immediately, he had to move onto Plan B: cajole.

There his plan hit a snag: he didn't even know her name and knew if he asked now he'd lose serious ground.

'So what do you say?'

She straightened, tossed her blonde ringlets over her shoulders with a flick of her hand and pinned him with a glare that spoke volumes before she opened her mouth.

'Thanks for the offer but my answer's no.'

CHAPTER TWO

LOLA didn't take kindly to being bossed around. She'd had enough of it growing up from her Miss Australia finalist mother and catwalk model sister.

Wear the boot cut jeans, not the slim fit.

Don't wear the A-line skirt; it makes your bum look big.

Use the coral lipstick, not the pink, you look washed out.

Bossiness never failed to put her back up and the moment Mr Tall, Dark and Domineering had strutted into her domain, ignoring house rules, she'd been primed for battle.

Mobile phones didn't belong in Go Retro for a reason. Trying to recreate a vintage ambience was imperative to her business and considering those infernal devices weren't invented back then, she'd made it a house rule to not have them used in the shop that was her pride and joy.

She also hated their constant buzzing and ringing and clattering as people tapped at those miniature keypads as if their lives depended on it.

How anyone could be glued to a phone when surrounded by all this beauty... She trailed a hand over a velvet nineteen-forties vermillion ball gown, savouring the plushness, the timeless elegance, let her fingers skim a floral silk scarf she bet could tell a few stories about the necks it had been knotted around over the years.

She glanced at the diamanté shoe clips, the crimson lipsticks in different brands, the fascinators at jaunty angles on the classically dressed mannequins.

Every item had been lovingly chosen in the hope it would bring joy to its next owner in the same way it had brought her joy to discover it. Surrounded by all these wonderful treasures of the past, how could anyone not be tempted?

'I need an answer.'

Just like that she snapped out of her reverie and glared at the philistine who wouldn't appreciate vintage at its finest if it slithered off a mannequin and onto his rather impressive frame.

The same impressive frame that made her want to run and hide out in the back room and let Immy deal with him. His type scared the beejeebies out of her: slick, smooth, successful. Guys who had it all and knew how to wield their many God-given talents. Guys who could use their looks and success to bedazzle a girl like her. Guys like Bodey.

Annoyed she'd let her past creep into the present, and doubly annoyed that she'd showed a glimmer of her fear when this guy had strutted in here as if he owned the place, she squared her shoulders.

So he thought he could boss her into accepting his deal by throwing money around and sweetening it with a personal recommendation?

He had that look about him, the look of a man used

to getting his own way: designer, from the top of his perfectly cut chocolate-brown hair to the bottom of his Italian loafers and his five-figure charcoal suit cost more than the entire front display.

As for Dazzle, of course she'd heard of them. Anyone who lived in Melbourne knew of the entertainment company's formidable reputation. You wanted something to make your event special? Dazzle did it, from jugglers to fire-eaters to international rock bands.

So he was the CEO? Figured. A guy like him would be used to throwing his weight around and never accepting a knock-back. Well, there was a first time for everything.

He wanted an answer? She had one for him, as soon as she phrased it in more ladylike terms than the ones running through her head, something along the lines of *stick it.*

Her disdain for his high-handedness must've shown for he rubbed a hand over his face and when it dropped, his haughty expression had been replaced by a rueful smile.

'Look, I'm sorry for barging in here and blustering. It's a sign of a desperate man.'

With those devastatingly blue eyes, charismatic smile and smoother-than-honey voice, she seriously doubted this guy had ever been desperate in his life.

Taking her silence as encouragement to continue, he held his hands out to her in supplication.

'My sister's getting married. She's this incredible, infuriating, adorable bundle of contradiction and I owe her a lot. She deserves the best and she loves this old stuff so I thought I'd organise this as a surprise.'

Great. If those baby-blues twinkling with sincerity weren't bad enough, the hint of a sweet guy beneath his steely tone as he sang his sister's praises undid her resolve to tell him where he could shove his crazy offer.

'When's she getting married?'

'Six weeks. A no frills private affair, which is why I want to spoil her with this.'

'No bridesmaids to organise it?'

He shook his head. 'She hasn't got the time for all that *faff* apparently. Too busy.'

His guilty look-away glance implied he knew all too well what that was like and the fact he was taking time out to organise a hen's night for his sister when it was probably the last thing on his all important phone's calendar made a big impression.

As if his six-two lean frame and blue eyes and charming smile hadn't already done that.

'She's a corporate lawyer: driven, obstinate, workaholic.'

She hazarded a guess the bride-to-be wasn't the only one in his family to boast those qualifications.

'She's always loved this old stuff and when I caught her flipping through a magazine last week, sighing over some charm school article run by a vintage shop owner in England, I thought it'd be a great wedding gift.'

Okay, she admitted it. His sister sounded like a perfect candidate for a Go Retro party. But that was just it. She'd done birthday parties, a few hours of escapism for ladies who shared her passion. She'd garnered rave reviews but this guy wasn't talking an afternoon. He wanted to hire her for a week?

'Cari would really love this a hell of a lot more than

any espresso machine or matching iPads, my only other gift ideas.'

He smiled again and this time, something unwelcome fluttered in her chest.

'So what do you say?'

She'd been set on saying no but his sincerity had got to her. From his description of his sister, she had this image in her head of a corporate businesswoman caught up in her whirlwind career, not having time to have a proper wedding with all the trimmings.

If this was the only luxury she'd get, a week out of her busy schedule to be pampered with a Go Retro hen's party she'd never forget, how could she say no?

As for his personal recommendation, no matter how hard she tried to ignore the mortgage papers strewn across her desk out the back, she couldn't. With the economy in a downslide, skyrocketing interest rates and conservative consumer spending were killing her business, despite its funky edge and appealing website and quality merchandise. If Go Retro didn't start making a bigger profit she'd have to shut up shop and that was one thing she couldn't even think about.

She'd worked too hard and too long to make her dream come true. No way would she give it up for the sake of pride.

Not wanting to give in too easily she named a price triple her hourly rate multiplied by seven, expecting him to barter.

He didn't.

'I can write you a cheque or wire the deposit directly into your business account now.' His lips quirked. 'If you'll give me back my phone, that is.'

His gaze dropped to her hips and she gripped the counter, trying not to squirm.

She may have lost weight since her teenage years and learned to highlight her good assets while minimising the bad but having her body scrutinised, especially by a hot guy, never failed to make her old inadequacies flare.

Were her hips too wide? Her waist too thick? Her butt too big? While the vintage fashion she embraced made the most of her curves, having a guy like him study her made her want to duck behind the counter.

She'd had her fair share of admiring glances from men before: it was what could develop from those glances that had her skittish despite being in the place she felt most comfortable.

'You do have it hidden away in that skirt of yours? Or have you performed some fancy trick and confiscated it for good?'

Her hand dived into her deep pocket and fumbled around for it, eager to hand it over and stop that potent blue-eyed gaze burning a hole in the metallic threaded eyelet lace of her favourite full-skirted polka dot dress.

'Here.'

As she handed it over their fingers brushed and a jolt akin to an electrical surge shot up her arm and zapped her in places that hadn't been zapped in a long, *long* time.

Not good.

The guys she occasionally dated were as far removed from this guy as her vintage dress from his designer suit. Arty guys, musicians, laid-back guys who liked a

Bohemian lifestyle far removed from the pressures of modern life.

Those were the type of guys who attracted her. Not career-driven, wealthy guys who could schmooze anyone into doing anything with their natural charms.

She should know. She'd tried one on for size once and was still wishing she'd got a refund while she could.

'Thanks.'

If that brief touch of fingertips hadn't been bad enough, his genuine smile made her knees quake ever so slightly and she hid her nerves behind snappiness.

'I don't even know your name,' she said, fiddling with the baskets of hair clips on the counter, rearranging them in carefully constructed disorder.

'Chase Etheridge.'

He held out his hand and she swallowed, silently cursing her stupidity. Of course he'd want to do the polite thing and shake hands. Something she could've coped with at any other time but hot on the heels of her bizarre reaction a few moments ago? Trouble.

'Lola Lombard.'

'Lovely name.'

His gaze locked on hers and held. 'Beautiful.'

And as she reluctantly placed her hand in his, and his fingers curled over hers, firm and warm and comforting, she almost believed for a fleeting second she was.

CHAPTER THREE

IN DESPERATE need of a calming cup of chamomile tea, Lola had just flicked the kettle switch on when Imogen breezed back in from her break, her face flushed as she clasped her hands to her chest.

'Was that *the* Chase Etheridge just leaving?'

She craned her neck, trying to get a last glimpse while Lola wrinkled her nose, more than happy to see the back of him.

'What was he doing here? He is sooo hot! Melbourne's most eligible bachelor for the third year running. No wonder, with those blue eyes, all year round tan, great smile, broad chest, cute butt—'

'Enough all ready.'

The last thing she needed right now was for her co-worker to list the guy's impressive attributes. Sadly, she'd noted them in minute detail herself and her nerves hadn't recovered despite him exiting the building.

Imogen sighed, her green eyes twinkling as she clapped her hands. 'Spill. What was he doing here?'

For a moment she wanted to tease her best friend but no way would Immy believe for one second that Chase was here on anything other than business. As if a guy like him would be interested in a girl like her for any other reason.

'He wants to use our services.'

'I can help service—'

'His sister's getting married and he wants Go Retro to do the hen's night.'

'Cool.'

Imogen edged into the tiny kitchen, grabbed her favourite 'I'm too sexy' mug and placed it next to hers. 'While you're weaving your magic with the hen and her posse, I'll entertain Chase.'

Imogen did a little shimmy as she spooned decaf into her cup. 'This is going to be fun.'

'It is,' Lola said, biting back a smile. 'Though this gig's a bit different.'

'How so?' Imogen added a shoulder wiggle to her hip shimmy. 'Does Chase need me to sleep over? Do some serious preparation for the hen's night? Because I'll do it, you know. I'm that kind of gal, totally dedicated to getting the job done whatever's required and—'

'Not you. Me.'

Lola often had to interrupt her friend mid-sentence otherwise the simplest of questions elicited a five minute long response.

This time, she enjoyed the confusion crinkling Immy's brow.

'You?'

The kettle clicked off and she poured boiling water into their cups.

'I'm the one that'll be staying over.'

Immy's jaw dropped, her mouth a perfect crimson glossed circle.

Enjoying her friend's momentary silence—it wouldn't last long—she dangled the chamomile bag.

'Apparently he's willing to pay for the privilege of having Go Retro run a week-long hen's party for his sis, no expenses spared, so while I'm doing that you'll be running the shop here.'

Imogen snapped her mouth shut into a mutinous line.

'Come on, Immy, we're a team. I run the workshops, you run this place when I'm not around. It works.'

The corners of Imogen's mouth twitched. 'Yeah, I know, but the thought of you rather than me getting up close and personal with that scrummy bachelor of the year makes me greener than Kermit.'

'I won't be getting up close and personal with anyone.'

Let alone an overconfident, overbearing workaholic who wouldn't know a hatbox from a pin curl. They had absolutely nothing in common and the fact she was even thinking along these lines meant she needed to get back to work before Immy made her more nervous.

And she was nervous, terrified in fact, for she'd agreed to meet Chase in a few hours to run through a proposed itinerary.

Her nerves had nothing to do with a lack of confidence in her work and everything to do with her irrational, erratic physical reaction to a guy who made her pulse race just by looking at her.

Imogen winked and tapped the side of her nose.

'Sure, you're going to concentrate on work and forget the fact Melbourne's hottest bachelor is looking over your shoulder. Just think, all those one on one consultations to ensure the hen's party runs smoothly, all those late night meetings, all those cosy chats to—'

'Don't you have mannequins to dress?'

Imogen's grin widened. 'Oh yeah, you're just dying to do this.'

She was dying all right but not for the reason Immy thought. While this may be just another job on paper the reality was far different. People like Chase, who moved in moneyed circles, had different expectations to the rest of them. What if the service she provided wasn't good enough? What if she wasn't good enough?

And that was bothering her the most, that she'd be found wanting in the same disheartening, discouraging, confidence sapping way she had been every day growing up.

'Want some help planning your wardrobe?'

Lola took a sip of tea and sighed with pleasure. 'Don't you mean the wardrobe for the party?'

Imogen cupped her mug and raised an eyebrow over the rim.

'Honey, you're likely to run into the sexiest guy in Melbourne on a regular basis for a week straight. Who cares what dress ups the brats play around with? It's you who needs to dazzle.'

Dazzle.

Her hands trembled as she clutched her cup more tightly. The thought of meeting Chase at Dazzle, his workplace, in a few hours set loose a bunch of rampaging butterflies on speed in her belly.

Taking a few sips of her soothing tea and finding it did nothing for her increasingly prevalent nerves she tipped the rest in the sink and rinsed the cup.

'Can you hold the fort for the next hour while I nip upstairs and do some serious planning for this party?'

'Sure, it'll be good practice for when I hold the fort on my own for a week while you're swanning around with chiselled Chase.'

'It's not like that,' she said, managing a wry smile at the thought of her swanning around with a guy like Chase.

Imogen cocked a hip as she leaned against the fridge. 'Then what's it like?'

'I'll let you know by the end of the week,' she said, her grin widening as Immy stuck out her tongue, the sound of childish smooching noises following her as she headed for the stairs.

Chase stared at his computer screen, trying to assimilate an inordinate amount of nonsensical information from the Go Retro website in an effort to be prepared for this meeting with Lola.

But the harder he tried to concentrate, the more the words blurred before his eyes, his attention constantly snagged by a small picture of Go Retro's proprietor in the top right hand corner.

A scoop-necked cherry dress cinched at the waist hugged her hourglass figure in all the right places, her hair falling in soft golden waves around a heart-shaped face dominated by those big brown eyes and ruby-slicked lips.

She looked incredible; and the picture didn't do her justice.

Lola Lombard in the flesh was something else.

He should know. He'd spent the last few hours

replaying their encounter: the way her lips pursed when she wasn't pleased, the feisty way she'd snatched his phone, the nervous flick of her tongue when she damped her lips when their fingers touched.

She was *so* not his type but there'd been a moment in that shop, surrounded by all those bows and whistles he'd wanted her to be.

The intercom on his desk buzzed and he clicked back onto his home screen. Lola Lombard had distracted him enough for one day.

'What is it, Jerrie?'

'Your sister to see you.'

'Send her in.'

He loved the way Cari dropped by to see him despite her manic schedule and today he was especially glad. She may not want a fancy wedding but he'd make sure she enjoyed his gift.

He stood and made it halfway across his office before she strode into the room, her black business suit crease-less, her hair and make-up immaculate for someone who'd hit the courts ten hours earlier.

He'd always been immensely proud of Cari and all she'd achieved and while she was getting married he couldn't help but wonder if she was slotting in her marriage among the rest of her appointments in the meticulous diary she kept.

'Hey, sis. Glad you could make it.'

He kissed her cheek, smiling when she barely paused en route to his desk, where she started searching it.

'Where's this surprise you mentioned on the phone?'

'Ah...so that's why you dropped in. And here I was,

thinking you missed seeing your amazing brother who you haven't had time for all week.'

'I don't have time for this so cut to the chase.'

She tempered her brisk tone with a cheeky smile, the same one she'd given him every time she used the well worn phrase; she'd been telling him to cut to the chase for a long time now.

'Fine. I won't bore you with details so here's the low-down.'

He perched on his desk, enjoying himself immensely. 'You know how you've cleared your schedule for a month for the wedding?'

'Yeah, I don't know how Hugh talked me into that.' She blew out an exasperated little huff but the corners of her mouth curving into a smile belied her belligerence. Hugh Hoffman was the only guy who'd come close to taming his strong-willed sister and it had been nothing short of a miracle that he'd coerced her into taking a whole month off from her precious job.

'I've talked to Hugh and he's given me the go-ahead to snaffle a week of your time.'

She frowned and glared at him over the top of her rimless spectacles.

'Not that Hugh has any say in what I do and how I spend my time, but what are you raving on about?'

Grinning, he spun around his computer screen. 'I'm throwing you a hen's party, sis. Not just a night, a whole week's worth.'

'You're insane…' The rest of her protest died on her lips as she focused on the screen, the spark of interest obvious as she caught sight of the Go Retro home page.

'Wow, check out those clothes,' she murmured, edging closer to the screen, squinting to get a better look.

'You will be,' he said, pulling up two chairs so they could sit. 'I know you love this old stuff and you'd never take time out to check it out yourself so I'm kidnapping you and that ratbag motley crew you call friends and locking you away in my Mount Macedon place for a week, with Go Retro throwing you a hen's bash you'll never forget.'

Dragging her gaze away from the screen, she stared at him with wide eyes.

'I take it back. You're not insane. You're certifiable. How on earth… Where did you get the idea… I don't believe this…'

He laughed at her lack of words, something his garrulous sister never had a problem with.

'Consider it my wedding present to you.'

He jerked his thumb at the screen, relieved when she bought his distraction. She'd honed that death glare to a fine art as a kid and it had been perfected with age. 'You and Hugh have everything, so this is a special something you'd never buy yourself.'

When she didn't speak, trepidation shot through him. Cari was his only sibling, the only person on the planet he truly cared about and he'd do anything to make her happy.

She'd done so much for him growing up: giving him a home, some semblance of family, when their parents were too busy indoctrinating their students rather than caring for the kids they had waiting futilely for them at home every night.

How many nights had they made macaroni cheese together, studied together, watched Tom and Jerry reruns until sleep had claimed them and their folks still hadn't made it home from Melbourne University? Too many and their closeness was as much about enforced dependency as blood ties.

'Come on, sis, say something.'

This time when she looked at him, every muscle in his body relaxed, for those weren't tears of anger in her eyes. They were tears of joy.

'This is the most brilliant gift anyone has ever given me and I can't thank you enough.'

She launched herself into his arms and hugged him until he could barely breathe, the two of them laughing as they disentangled.

'So I get to play dress ups with all that gorgeous gear for a week?'

'Yeah, and a whole bunch of other stuff, which I'll tell you about once I get the itinerary straight with Lola.'

'Lola?'

He deliberately kept his tone devoid of any emotion; too little too late if Cari's quirked eyebrow was any indication.

'Lola Lombard, the owner. She'll be running your hen's party.'

Cari's astute gaze bored into him. 'Can't believe a woman who owns a shop like that would take a week out of her schedule to run a private party.'

'It's part of her business, running parties.'

Along with her sideline of pilfering phones and distracting men.

'Uh-huh.' Cari tapped her bottom lip with a perfectly

manicured fingernail. 'Why do I get the feeling you're not telling me everything?'

'Because you're naturally suspicious?'

Swivelling the screen back towards him, he shut down the notebook.

'So now you know the big secret you can head back to your glass office in the sky and sue a few more corporations.'

When she opened her mouth to protest, he held up a finger.

'But remember, a fortnight from today, get ready to party.'

With a rueful smile, she patted his cheek and sailed out the door, her fingers already glued to her smartphone as she checked for emails from clients.

They were so alike: busy, driven, ambitious, thriving on the challenge of business at a high level.

The lawyer and the CEO; as far removed from their parents, the English Lit professors, as could be.

He often wondered if that was what drove them—the unspoken urge to be nothing like the parents who hadn't given a toss about them.

It sure had spurred him on, to enter an industry filled with fun and parties and light-heartedness, as far removed from his sterile childhood and his parents' academic snobbery.

Not that he and Cari ever discussed it. Instead, they paid the obligatory visits at birthdays and Christmases, made perfunctory small talk with the people who were more strangers than family, before escaping for another few months.

Though not a strained visit went by without him

wishing they'd show some interest: in his career, his success, his life. Futile wishes, considering his folks continued to be absorbed by their students, their time-tables and themselves, in that order.

Whatever the motivation driving himself and Cari he was proud of how far they'd come and, swiping a hand over his face, he flipped up the screen with the other, instantly drawn to Lola's picture again.

Time to concentrate on more important matters; like seeing what luscious Lola Lombard could come up with for Cari's hen's party.

And getting a grip on why she held such an unwanted fascination for him.

CHAPTER FOUR

LOLA clutched her monstrous cerise crushed velvet holdall against her chest as she strode along Collins Street.

While the Dazzle offices might be at the elegant bustling *Paris* end of the street, walking through the central business district after dark always made her nervous.

The fairy lights strung through tree branches twinkled as commuters rushed past her, heading for the underground train stations, oblivious to their surroundings, caught up in the rat race.

She eased her grip on her bag and tucked it under her arm, her fear receding. Being a business drone like these commuters was far scarier to her than any imagined bogeymen lurking in the shadows.

She hated that lifestyle: the pace, the relentlessness, the frenetic whirlwind to be bigger and better and brighter than everyone else.

She'd tried it once, had been caught up in it against her will. After all, what choice did she have when her mum was a former Miss Australia finalist and her sister a catwalk supermodel?

They'd dragged her along to countless parties and Fashion Weeks and make-up launches, no doubt hoping some of that glamour would rub off on her, the lacklustre fat Lombard of the trio.

While she'd enjoyed the fashion shows and make-up giveaways, she didn't belong in that world and never would. The fakeness, the schmoozing, the air kisses while everyone sized up everyone else behind their backs... Nah, she'd leave that to people who thrived on it, like her gorgeous waiflike sister Shareen—yeah, she was that famous she had a single name, like Cher and Madonna—and her mum, Darla, who still graced the glossy magazines every few weeks.

The sad thing was, she could now match them for poise and fashion-consciousness yet they rarely acknowledged her transformation, they were so caught up in their own lives. And what was worse? That she still cared what they thought, after all this time.

Just once, she'd like her mum to say, *Darling, you look gorgeous,* a compliment often thrown out to Shareen. The closest she got these days was, 'That's an interesting outfit,' which was better than nothing but not a patch on what she wanted, what she deserved.

Annoyed at dredging up memories guaranteed to sap her confidence, she picked up the pace and as she reached the offices of Dazzle, enclosed in a modern glass monstrosity reaching for the sky, she knew Chase Etheridge belonged in the group of go-getters she'd just shouldered through.

He oozed class that money couldn't buy, an innate assurance evident in those slashed cheekbones, square jaw and sensual mouth.

The way he'd barged into her shop, overpowering her personal space with his brand of charisma, never

doubting for a second she'd fall in line with his plans...
Yeah, he had confidence to burn and, despite her private
vow made a long time ago to never fall for the false-
ness of that glamorous world, she found herself looking
forward to seeing him again.

Irritated, she marched through the glass doors, ignoring the inevitable stares from business drones leaving
the building.

She was used to the stares, used to people taking a
second look when she walked past. Hadn't she cultivated
this image for that very reason all those years ago, turning her personal penchant for vintage into a unique look
all her own?

She liked being admired, liked standing out from
Shareen and Darla and the more people complimented
her the further she honed her image to the point where
she never stepped out of her bedroom without her retro
mask in place.

Lola Lombard was striking, different, distinctive and
a far cry from frumpy, mousy Louise Lombard who'd
slunk in her gorgeous family's footsteps, wishing she
could be just like them.

The ten second ride in a supersonic elevator made her
ears pop and, increasingly grumpy she strode along the
plush thirtieth floor corridor and into the flashy Dazzle
offices.

She'd expected glitz to the max but the understated
elegance of the place surprised her: cinnamon carpet,
mushroom walls and a simple mahogany front desk
bordered on antique. The whole front office had an old
world charm rather than the modern slant she'd expected
after meeting Chase and her misconception rattled her.

What other surprises did Chase Etheridge hide up his Armani sleeves?

A suitably sleek receptionist glanced up as she approached and to her credit the woman didn't balk or stare at her appearance, offering a genuine smile instead.

'Hi, you must be Lola. Chase is expecting you. Last door on the left; go straight in.'

Acutely aware of her nineteen-fifties dress next to the receptionist's black Dolce and Gabbana power suit, she headed off down the hallway where Miss D&G had pointed.

She hesitated outside a monstrous ebony door, wishing she didn't have to do this. Then she remembered that latest mortgage rise notification and her teetering finances, took a deep breath and raised her fist to knock.

Her knuckles had barely grazed the door when it opened and she bit back a wistful sigh.

Because that was how seeing Chase again made her feel: pensive, yearning for something she knew wasn't good for her yet craved anyway. Kind of like her favourite double choc fudge brownies.

'Glad you could make it.'

As if she'd had any choice. Apart from her dire financial straits, the minute he'd barged into Go Retro he would never have taken no for an answer; he was that kind of guy.

'I've got a rough presentation for you to take a look at.'

'Great, come on in.'

He opened the door wider but didn't move and as she slid past him she could've sworn a bolt of electricity zapped her. How else could she explain her wobbly knees and shaky hands and boneless spine?

Striding across the office as if she was used to being in fancy executive suites every day of the week, her eyes widened when she neared the desk, a gargantuan glass and chrome concoction that would've served half a call centre.

It was covered with fancy gadgets and neat document stacks, with a gleaming stainless steel pen holder housing gold pens. A laptop as thin as a wafer sat side by side with a huge PC screen bigger than her television.

The desk spoke volumes about Chase: modern, efficient, smooth. So what did her chipped, scratched antique roll top say about her?

'Have a seat.'

Oh-oh. She'd expected him to retreat behind his well organised desk and leave her a welcome few metres away on the other side. Instead, he gestured to a low ochre suede sofa nearby—a sofa without matching chairs, which meant he'd be sitting next to her, nice and cosy, while she gave her presentation.

When he cast a quizzical glance she perched on the edge of the sofa, smoothing her full skirt before delving into her bag for her notes, concentrating on gathering her documents and trying not to stiffen when he sat next to her, so temptingly close.

'Looks like you've got an office in that bag.'

'I like to be prepared,' she said, yanking the folder from her bag and brandishing it like a protective shield.

'Let me guess. You were in Girl Scouts.'

His mouth kicked into a teasing smile and she swore her heart kicked back.

'Not a chance.'

She'd been too busy traipsing around after her sister as a kid, fetching costumes and tights and mascara wands, hanging around backstage killing time at countless talent and fashion shows. While she'd loved the clothes she'd hated the condescending pity stares from people in the industry who knew she was Shareen's fat baby sister.

Exasperated she'd let more memories distract her at a time like this, she flipped open the folder.

'This is a very basic outline of the week, which I'll flesh out later...'

The rest of her pitch faded into oblivion as he leaned towards her to look at the folder, his shoulder brushing hers and setting off a bunch of internal fireworks that rocketed and pinwheeled and spiralled until she was dizzy.

This out of control physical reaction to a guy who embodied everything she didn't like was crazy, a purely hormonal reaction for a girl who hadn't had a date in a while. Okay, a long while.

Whatever the reason, it didn't make this any easier and, gritting her teeth against blue-eyed, wicked, smiling, rich rogues, she rattled the paper and stabbed her finger at the first point.

'The gist of the hen's party is pampering for the bride-to-be, including manicures, pedicures, facials, massages, makeovers. Then I throw in deportment lessons, etiquette, dance and home-style cooking classes.'

Chase snorted and she raised an eyebrow.

'The thought of Cari in the kitchen, let alone cooking anything beyond microwaving a frozen dinner is mind-boggling.'

'She doesn't cook at all?'

Lola never understood how anyone couldn't at least scramble eggs or make a basic chicken salad. She loved the warmth of a well-used, well-loved kitchen: the aromas, the fresh herbs, the spices, the fun of throwing stuff together and creating a delicious surprise.

Guess that explained why she'd been the size of a blimp growing up and her mum and sister never ventured to the fridge for more than to grab iced water and a lettuce leaf.

Chase grinned and once again her heart performed some weird dance ritual halfway between tap and mambo.

'Cari's a take-out kind of gal.'

He pointed at her presentation. 'So the cooking? This I've got to see.'

Her heart did a final pirouette and sank into the splits as she realised what that meant.

'You'll be at the house?'

A slight frown creased his brow and she silently cursed her abrupt question complete with horrified undertone.

'We'll see. I have enough work here to keep me busy so I'll be staying in town most likely.'

The guy had *two* houses? She could barely afford the mortgage on one. Another reason why she was here—the thought of her precious two bedroom Californian bungalow a street away from Go Retro being ripped away from her was too much to bear.

She'd put it up as collateral when she'd gone from leasing the Errol Street storefront to buying it as an investment in her business and now that interest rates were on the rise and consumer spending was down and Go Retro wasn't doing so well...

Panic flared, lurching from the darkest recesses where she clamped down on it on a daily basis, doing everything in her power to make Go Retro a roaring success and saving her business, her livelihood and her home.

'I've got a penthouse not far from here, but get away to the Mount Macedon house when I can.'

'Great.'

Her response sounded forced and before he could pick up on it, she rushed on. 'I'll need to know if there are any food allergies, that sort of thing.'

He nodded and slipped his trusty smartphone from his jacket pocket, tapping away at the miniature keyboard with his thumb.

'Onto it.'

His rudeness grated—stupid darn technology—and she wanted to rattle him.

'With the itinerary I've planned, including two six-course dinner parties, I might need to stay over two nights out of the seven.'

As if he'd care. He'd be ensconced in his glass tower in the city, giving her carte blanche to his mansion at Mount Macedon. And while his blasé attitude to his wealth annoyed her, she had to admit she couldn't wait to check out his country mansion.

'I'll make sure to be there those nights,' he said, his eyes twinkling with mischief and, to her mortification she blushed, only serving to increase his amusement as his mouth curved into a teasing smile.

Great, now he'd think she couldn't handle a little light-hearted flirtation.

The problem wasn't the flirting as much as the guy doing it. For a woman who hated his lifestyle and all it stood for—superficiality at its finest—she sure wasn't averse to the man himself.

Gathering her documents along with her wits, she shoved them back into the folder and stood.

'Well, that'll do for the preliminaries. I'll email you something more formal next week.'

'Sounds good.'

He stood and glanced at his watch. 'I need to be somewhere.'

Bristling at his careless dismissal, she squared her shoulders.

'I'll get out of your way then.'

Her frosty tone raised both his eyebrows.

'Actually, if you're not doing anything I'd love you to join me.'

If the sofa wasn't pressing against the back of her knees she would've crumpled into an embarrassing heap.

Speechless, she searched her brain for a polite refusal, something to mask her total shock he'd actually asked her out.

'There's some fashion designer/modelling agency launch, might be good PR for you to meet some people? They're always looking for a new angle for these shindigs, could be good for your business.'

His phone beeped and he cast a quick glance at it and grimaced.

'Plus you'll be doing me a huge favour seeing as I've just heard the media will be there and if I turn up to these things single they're always writing gutter rubbish about me the next day.'

'When you put it that way, how can a girl refuse?'

Her sarcasm wasn't lost on him and he shot her an apologetic glance while tapping a response on that infernal phone.

'Look, I really think it'll be a beneficial business opportunity for you and I offered to introduce you to suitable contacts as part of our deal.'

Hitting send on his phone, he finally gave her his full attention and, as the impact of those startling blue eyes and sensual lips curved, she almost wished he'd return to his phone.

'As for helping me out of a tight spot by being my date for a few hours, consider it your good deed for the day.'

Hating how he'd railroaded her, she folded her arms. 'Maybe I'm not feeling so charitable today.'

With his eyes crinkling adorably at the corners, he leaned towards her and she held her breath, bombarded by an incoming sexy male she had no hope of handling.

'Come on, Lola. My reputation is in your hands.'

She snorted, the corners of her mouth tugging into a reluctant smile. 'I have a feeling your reputation was shot long before I came along.'

'Ouch.'

He clasped his hands to his heart while hers gave a

suspicious twang; enough of a wake up call to never take anything he said seriously. Chase schmoozed for a living, knowing the right thing to say for any occasion.

However much he turned on the charm she had to realise it was as natural to him as breathing and not read too much into it, something she'd been guilty of before. Sometimes having dreams of a white picket fence and home cooked meals and a bundle of adorable kids wasn't so helpful, especially when smooth-talking guys like Bodey who she dated more than a few times started to look like a prospective groom.

'Shall I take your silence as agreement?'

She shook her head at his good-natured persistence. 'You can take my silence as musing time filled with misgivings.'

'But you'll do it anyway, right?'

She hated accepting help from anyone, least of all a guy like Chase who she suspected of having *strings* attached to his offer but she couldn't bypass the opportunity to put Go Retro front and centre with fresh contacts. New business meant a much needed cash injection and it wouldn't be smart to rely on pride alone to save her.

While her head screamed no, her hopeful heart already strutted alongside him, proud to be his date for a few hours.

Exhaling on an exaggerated sigh, she shrugged. 'Why not?'

Giving a much needed boost to her business and playing Chase's arm candy for an evening? She could think of worse ways to spend a few hours.

'Thanks, you're a lifesaver,' he said, brushing a quick

kiss on her cheek, already distracted by an incoming call while she stood there, reeling.

Not from the quick thank you peck as much as how it made her feel.

As if she wanted a lot more where that came from.

CHAPTER FIVE

THE moment Lola stepped into the strategically lit loft she knew she'd made a mistake.

This was *so* not her scene.

Rake-thin models, slick corporate suits, elite sport stars, the cream of Melbourne's A-list mingled and schmoozed and air kissed in a scene so reminiscent of her past she froze.

But this party wasn't the worst of it. Oh, no, the car ride from Dazzle to here with Chase flirting with practised determination had shot her nerves to pieces before she set foot in this place.

Some hotshot party she could handle. It was handling the hotshot himself that had her in a real tizz.

Chase cast a quick concerned glance her way before placing a hand in the small of her back and gently propelling her into the throng, nodding and smiling like a professional but moving all the while, determinedly cutting a path to the other side of the loft where a quiet pocket of low slung leather sofas framed an L-shaped corner.

Grateful for the reprieve while she regrouped her shattered resistance to sexy, smooth, utterly gorgeous guys, she sank onto a sofa.

'Would you like a drink?'

What she would like was to get the hell out of here and away from him but the thought of her skyrocketing mortgage and dwindling bank account forced her to smile and nod.

'Sure, a lime soda would be great.'

He saluted. 'Coming right up.'

He headed for the bar, as trendy and sleek as the loft's occupants, running the length of one wall. Chase blended with the hip crowd, another gorgeous guy in a designer suit with a winning smile and a trillion dollar bank account. He fitted in while she stood out like a pin curl on a twenty-first century model.

She glanced down at her skirt, at the hint of tulle petticoat peeping out from beneath, loving the fullness it created, the fun flare, the white polka dots stark against an ebony background.

Dresses like this spoke to her. They whispered stories of the beautiful women who'd worn them many decades earlier, of a time when women's curves were embraced, not ridiculed. Such a special era...and so far removed from the present to be laughable.

Looking around at the stylish women in the crowd, swathed in head to toe clingy black, she doubted they'd ever had to battle bullies at school who'd tormented them over their lunch boxes, count calories under a beauty queen mother's watchful eye or hide backstage and pretend to be another lackey at a supermodel sister's catwalk show.

Not that she was jealous exactly but she envied them their carefree 'togetherness', as if they knew their place in the world, taking for granted their easy self-assurance.

She'd worked hard for her confidence, worked at it on a daily basis; with every wave of the mascara wand over her naturally pale lashes, with every tuck of her curls, with every slash of her signature Crash Crimson lipstick, she put together an image to the world. An image that showed a confident businesswoman who loved anything vintage, who enhanced her assets and made the most of the curves she'd once hidden.

But sitting here in this trendy loft, surrounded by Melbourne's A-list, she recognised her confidence was as brittle as her bank balance.

And it was all because of the man striding through the crowd towards her, that roguish smile directed solely at her, unsettling her far more than the hip crowd.

'Here you go.'

Chase appeared from the left and handed her a drink. 'Everything okay?'

'Why wouldn't it be?'

He studied her face and she quickly schooled it into the bright, bubbly mask she used to greet customers.

'You were looking mighty pensive when I was grabbing these.'

He'd been watching her? She tried to hide her surprise. In a room of wall to wall revealing outfits and glamorous women he'd been eyeing her?

'Guess I've just revealed my hand,' he said, his smile rueful as indecision flashed across his face for a second then cleared.

Before she knew what was happening, he'd taken hold

of her hand in a firm, warm grip that sent excitement ricocheting through her.

'I have to tell you, Lola, you fascinate me.'

If she'd been any other girl, a whole host of witty replies would've tripped from her lips, making him laugh and easing the awkwardness of the moment.

As it was, she sat there, stunned, hoping her jaw hadn't dropped as she frantically searched for a suitable response other than, *Say it again.*

She hated feeling this uncertain, this panicky. It reminded her of being put on the spot countless times in her past when she never had the right reply or frustratingly thought up something witty to say hours later.

Chase made her nervous and she'd spent an eternity battling her anxiety in social situations, honing her confident mask to project an assured image to the world and enhance her business. Sadly, the more attention Chase paid her, the more cracks appeared in that carefully constructed mask.

To her relief, he smoothed over her gaucheness with a slow, sexy smile that tied her tongue into a thousand more knots.

'I know you think I'm crazy for saying that after only meeting you earlier today but I'm blunt in business and it tends to spill over into other areas of my life.'

He paused, squeezed her hand gently before lifting it to his lips and brushing a soft kiss across the back of it. 'You'll get to know that about me.'

She would?

As her hand tingled with the delicious touch of his lips, she reacted how she always did in a situation like this.

Floundering way out of her depth, she grabbed her handbag, mumbled an, 'I'll be right back,' and made a mercy dash to the loo.

Only to be waylaid a moment later by some grey-haired guy in a maroon suit with a thin leather tie that came from the same era as some of her merchandise.

She'd planned on giving him the brush-off, needing time to reassemble her wits after Chase's declaration, the frightening, exhilarating *'you fascinate me'* still ringing in her ears, until he introduced himself and she recognised Arledge Hahndorf as being a major player in Melbourne's money world.

In that moment, with the top actuary shaking her hand, she took a steadying breath, ignored the internal mess of quivering nerves thanks to Chase's serious flirtation, and gave the guy her most dazzling smile.

How many times had she charmed clients and wooed business with her practised poise? Too many to count and meeting Arledge Hahndorf was just like that—a business opportunity too good to pass up.

She chatted and smiled and nodded as the actuary expounded his theories on Melbourne's money market, determinedly avoiding glancing at the sofa in the far corner of the loft.

She could handle the top money movers in the room, but handling Chase Etheridge at his devastating best was another matter entirely.

Chase loved these shindigs. Loved the buzz in a room full of movers and shakers, loved the deals clinched over Cosmopolitans and whisky sours, loved the aura of success that hung over the crowd like a rainbow of riches.

Yet there was something off-kilter about tonight and as Lola charmed Melbourne's top actuary he knew what it was.

In less than twenty-four hours this woman had made him feel something he hadn't felt in a long time: uncertainty.

There was something so wholesomely appealing about her, something so refreshing in her honest answers, her uncontrived responses to him, that he found himself drawn to her in a way that intrigued as well as terrified.

He loved women: loved dating them, entertaining them, spoiling them, but that was where it ended.

He didn't like them getting too close; close enough to make him feel anything other than admiration and lust. Yet in the space of a day Lola Lombard had inspired a hell of a lot more than that.

He'd never met anyone like her.

A woman of contrasts, she could swan through a room like this with her head held high, seemingly oblivious to the stares.

Yet when he'd complimented her, held her hand and kissed it, she'd bolted faster than his prized racehorse.

Taking a slug of his boutique beer, he watched her laugh at something the actuary said, a genuine laugh with cute crinkles at the corners of her eyes and a wide smile from those incredibly red, incredibly sensual lips and he wasn't sure whether the flip in his gut was from the beer or the power this woman could wield with a bat of her long lashes.

She chose that moment to dart a nervous glance his way and his gut tightened again. No doubt about it, he'd better tread carefully with this one.

He'd hired her for a week to make his sister happy. Maybe they could have a harmless flirtation, a fun interlude, too?

As he raised his beer glass in her direction in a silent toast, and the faintest blush stained her cheeks as she returned her attention to the actuary, that flicker of uncertainty gripped him harder.

Yeah, he needed to watch his step with Lola. No use letting a simple attraction affect his foolproof judgement. He'd once harboured foolish hopes, expecting more from people than they were ready to give.

Never again.

When she'd been younger Lola had often got swept along in other's plans.

Playing wardrobe co-ordinator to Shareen's many fashion shows? Yep.

Lugging make-up cases along with suitcases of shoes? Done that too.

Stuck at some phoney after-party pretending to pick at sushi when she was starving for a burger and shake? Too many times to count.

At the time it'd been easier to go with the flow than argue with her mum and by the time she'd grown a backbone it had been too late. Her bitterness at being the second string daughter had become ingrained.

She'd worked hard at building an inner confidence that no one could shake, had honed her smiles along with her wardrobe over the years, taking pride in how far she'd come from the subservient fat kid who would've done anything for praise.

So what was her excuse for letting Chase railroad her into this?

It had been tough enough accompanying him to that party, though she'd justified it as business. While she'd inwardly seethed with nerves courtesy of his twenty-four-seven charm, she'd met some useful people with potential contacts so it hadn't been all bad.

But this?

'Come in, make yourself at home.'

Easy for him to say as she hovered on the edge of his step-down lounge trying not to gawk at his penthouse.

She felt like Alice in Wonderland falling down the rabbit hole: floundering, astonished, way out of her depth.

'I'll make another call to Cari, see how long she'll be.'

She managed a mute nod, wondering how he could be so oblivious to all this gob-smacking luxury. Then again, he lived here, was used to it and probably took it for granted, while for her, seeing the sheer obscenity of the palace he lived in merely served to reinforce the yawning gap between them.

'Can I get you anything? Coffee? Drink?'

She shook her head, wishing he'd go make that call already for the faster his sister arrived and they did the whole introduction thing the faster she could escape.

'No, thanks, I'm fine.'

'If you change your mind, the kitchen's through there.'

He pointed over her right shoulder. 'I meant it when I said make yourself at home.'

'Thanks.'

Her smile felt as brittle as her grip on reality as he punched numbers into his phone and headed down a long hallway.

When he vanished into a room, she exhaled, slumping against the nearest wall and squeezing her eyes shut.

This had to be a dream, one of those weird alternate realities where everything was too perfect and when she woke up she'd be back to her ordinary life.

Not that there was anything wrong with her life, per se. In fact, she was pretty darn happy with all she'd achieved: leaving Brisbane behind to start a new life in Melbourne, striking out on her own, reinventing herself, making Go Retro a reality.

Yeah, her life was pretty darn fantastic but she'd be lying if she didn't admit to wishing for a special someone to share it with.

She had a fair idea of her dream guy too: creative, laid-back, artistic. The opposite of Bodey.

And the complete antithesis of Chase Etheridge.

Yet here she was, in his penthouse, seriously swooning over more than his antique armoire which looked strangely out of place amongst all the clean, modern white furniture.

Stepping down into the lounge she headed for the armoire, ran a hand over the exquisite polished wood. Her fingertips grazed several chips but rather than detract they added character to the piece.

She'd love something like this in her place, with its polished restored floorboards, alabaster walls she'd painted herself and retro furniture she'd scoured from markets across Melbourne. A place so far removed from Chase's slick penthouse they may as well be on different planets.

If the man himself was her polar opposite, their respective abodes reinforced it.

Her North Melbourne Californian bungalow channelled a bygone era, filled with vintage appliances interspersed with antiques. Her collections overflowed into every room—hairpins, hat boxes, compacts, shoe clips—she loved the artfully decorated clutter, the warmth, the cosiness.

While this place… Glancing around, she suppressed a shiver, for this pristine penthouse with its clinical white sofas and glass coffee tables and strategically hidden plasmas didn't give a hint of warmth.

Except the armoire…

It snagged her attention again as she wondered what a guy like Chase would be doing with an old piece like this.

'Cari's on her way.'

She jumped and tried to hide the fact he'd startled her by leaning against the armoire, belatedly realising she must look like some advertisement torn from the pages of a decades old newspaper.

Hating how uncertain she felt around him, she straightened and tapped the armoire.

'This is gorgeous.'

To her surprise his expression closed off. 'If you like that sort of thing.'

'You must if it's sitting in your lounge.'

For the first time all evening he stared at her with anything but warmth.

'A sentimental mistake.'

He stepped into the lounge and headed for the floor to ceiling glass windows overlooking a glittering Melbourne many storeys below.

'How much do we tell Cari? Do you want to run through the itinerary or keep it as a surprise?'

His abrupt change of subject was almost as surprising as the sudden remoteness that radiated off him like a protective force field.

He didn't want to talk about the armoire and in asking about it she'd inadvertently stepped into an emotional minefield.

Maybe she'd been wrong about him. Maybe there was a heart behind that cool, uber professional exterior.

Shoving her curiosity aside, she joined him at the windows.

'More fun for Cari if it's a surprise, I think.'

He nodded, his expression pensive as he turned towards her.

'Good idea. She always loved surprises as a kid.'

Buoyed by his thawing, she said, 'You two were close?'

'Yeah.'

She heard warmth in that one word, warmth and closeness and love. The way she saw it, not many brothers would take time out from their busy schedules to organise a surprise like this for their sisters.

The fact he'd noted what Cari liked, storing her love of vintage in his memory banks from a chance comment from a magazine, said a lot. And the fact he'd taken the time to find her shop, follow up and organise a week long hen's party really put him right up there with best brother status.

What would it be like to be close to a sibling? To share a real bond, a love that went beyond blood ties.

She wouldn't know. Her relationship with Shareen revolved around strained silences at the dinner table on the rare occasions the Lombards got together.

The moment she'd stopped being Shareen's whipping girl, PA and dresser was the moment Shareen had turned her back on her once and for all.

They had nothing in common, never had. Her mum and Shareen were more like sisters, an observation made repeatedly during Shareen's early modelling days by many people in the industry, while she'd been virtually invisible.

She'd liked going unnoticed, slipping beneath the radar while people, including her parents, fawned over her sister. It was when they'd turned their meddling make-over ways on her that her life had become a misery.

She'd weathered their fussing, their interference in her life from her diet to her clothes and now that she had her own style, her own success, they still treated her as if she came a distant second—something that mattered more than it should.

'Do you have any siblings?'

'One, a sister.'

She waited for him to ask who she was, what she did, were they close but thankfully the buzzer sounded, giving her a much needed reprieve.

She didn't want to talk about her supermodel sister,

didn't want Chase's eyes widening with admiration then quickly narrowing with assessment as he inevitably compared her with the gorgeous worldwide phenomenon that was Shareen and found her lacking.

And that would hurt more than she'd like to admit for in the space of a day she'd come to value what Chase thought of her.

She liked that he flirted with her. She liked that he admired her. And she really liked that he found her fascinating.

How long would that last if he discovered she was a distant second to the stunning Shareen?

When Cari breezed into the room Lola tried not to do a double take. From the top of her immaculately styled mahogany-streaked hair to the bottom of her designer suit trousers, she was like a female version of Chase.

'Hi, you must be Lola.'

Even her handshake was like her brother's, strong and brisk, and while Lola knew she shouldn't be intimidated something about this businesswoman rattled her, as if she'd see right through her.

Then Cari smiled and the genuine warmth she saw there went a long way to settling her nerves.

Donning the smile she used to greet customers, she said, 'Lola Lombard, your hostess for the hen's week.'

To her amazement, Cari clapped her hands and did a little jig on the spot.

'I know! I can't believe my brother organised all this but I can't wait.'

Cari's excited gaze swept over her and she stiffened, an old habit born from years of scrutiny, but there was no judgement here.

'I have to say, I absolutely love your dress. It's gorgeous! Is it an original?'

Buoyed by Cari's gushing—if she was this excited about a dress, wait until she saw what she had in store for her at her hen's party—Lola nodded.

'It's a favourite. I picked it up online, unworn, from the daughter of an old dancer who'd stored all these new dresses away in the attic, decades ago.'

'That must've been some find.'

'It was. I'll bring the rest along; you can check them out.'

Cari's eyes widened like a true aficionado. 'That'd be great. I've always wanted to own one, though goodness knows where I'd wear it.'

She grimaced, waved a hand at her suit. 'I'm stuck in these all day every day.'

'Ahem.' Chase cleared his throat and they both swivelled towards him, Cari chuckling at his pained expression while she bit back a grin.

'As much as I'm glad you two are hitting it off, all this talk of frocks is making me cringe.'

Cari snorted. 'Don't mind him. He's just used to being the centre of attention.'

Cari nudged her as if they'd been friends for ever and once gain Lola marvelled at what it would've been like to have a sibling like either of the Etheridges.

'Can't handle being upstaged, that's his problem.'

Chase waved his arms in the air. 'Hello! I'm still here.'

'Not for long.' Cari waved him towards the kitchen. 'Why don't you make yourself useful and go whip us up a couple of espressos?'

Lucky she liked strong coffee for Lola had a feeling no one could stop Cari when she was in full steamroller mode.

'And rustle up a couple of Anzac bikkies while you're at it. We're starving.'

Bemused by Cari's take charge attitude and even more amazed by Chase's capitulation, Lola wondered what the corporate dynamo would come up with next.

The moment Chase left the room, she didn't wait long to find out.

Cari clutched her arm, her voice barely above a whisper. 'So what's going on with you and my brother?'

Heck. If the last few minutes hadn't confounded her, that blunt question would've done the trick.

'Nothing. He came into my shop earlier today and hired me to run your hen's party. That's it.'

'Like hell.'

Cari released her, only to fold her arms and pin her with a sceptical glare that must intimidate her clients to great effect.

'I'm a good judge of character, Lola. We've only just met and I like you.'

She paused, her eyes narrowing as she moved in for the kill.

'But let me be perfectly blunt. My brother dates vapid women with IQs on a par with their shoe size. He doesn't take them to industry parties on the first night they meet and he never, ever brings them home.'

She took a step towards her and Lola tried not to shrink back in fear like a criminal with secrets to hide.

'So while you may not be technically classed as his

date because he's hired you for my hen's party, let me tell you that Chase likes you. Otherwise you wouldn't be here.'

Cari waved her perfectly manicured hands around and Lola spotted an antique charm bracelet semi-hidden beneath her jacket cuff. Considering her corporate wardrobe, it must be the lawyer's one concession to her love of vintage.

Hoping to distract, she said, 'Nice bracelet. I may have some charms at the shop I can bring along too.'

'Thanks, that'd be great.'

Cari darted a glance over her shoulder in the direction of the kitchen before beckoning her closer. 'I love this old stuff. Which is why I wear vintage under here too.'

She tugged at her shirt collar and Lola hoped she didn't blush. Go Retro had its fair share of old style lingerie but customers were rarely so forthcoming.

'Now, let's get back to the question of you and my brother.'

More than a little stunned by Cari's full-on approach, Lola quickly scrambled for a response, knowing she had to say something to avoid being railroaded into blurting exactly what was going on here: that while this was all business to Chase—his natural flirting notwithstanding—she was fast developing a crush on the hen's brother.

Did that make him a rooster?

The ridiculous question popped into her head and she stifled a giggle, not helping her cause when Cari caught sight of her twitching lips.

'A-ha! I knew there's something going on. You're looking all coy and Chase looked dazed when I came in.'

She rubbed her hands together like a Machiavellian puppet master yanking their strings.

'This is too good. Wait till I ask Chase—'

'Ask me what?'

Lola's heart gave a frightening ka-thump as he strolled back into the room bearing a tray with their coffees, milk, sugar and cookies. He should've looked odd performing such a domestic task in his business suit but he didn't. He looked like a guy comfortable enough in his own skin to perform any task.

Leaping in before Cari could embarrass her further, she sent the woman she'd only just met—and her client technically—a warning glare.

'Cari was just asking about the itinerary for the hen's week but I said it was a surprise so she wanted to grill you.'

Chase's shrewd stare darted between the two of them. He didn't buy her cover-up but thankfully he didn't push it.

'Sorry, sis. All one big surprise.'

'I bet,' Cari murmured, raising an eyebrow at her across the rim of her coffee cup.

Desperate to change the subject, Lola dumped way too much sugar into her coffee and stirred vigorously, the spoon clanking against the cup a dead giveaway of her increasing nervousness.

'Have you confirmed with your friends? What kind of numbers are we looking at?'

There, a perfectly legitimate business question to get

them back on track and away from the dicey subject of her presence in Chase's life.

'Just me and my four closest colleagues.'

Lola almost choked on her coffee. *Colleagues?* Didn't she mean friends?

Annoyingly intuitive, Chase piped up. 'Sadly, all my sister's friends are workaholic drones like her, that's why she calls them colleagues.'

Fire flashed in Cari's deep blue eyes so like her brother's. 'At least I have friends.'

Chase shrugged, his grin widening as Lola wondered how many times over the years the siblings had played this game.

If they were so alike in personality and ambition it stood to reason they'd be fiery too, baiting each other to see how fast the other could snap.

And while she never would've had the spunk for something like this, she almost wished she'd had a sister to trade banter with.

Shareen had been a master at baiting; out of cruelty rather than fun. She'd picked on her clothes, her hair, her weight, her social skills, not necessarily in that order and she'd always lamented the fact that while her sister may have been beautiful on the outside it certainly hadn't extended within.

'Do we need to bring anything, Lola?'

She shook her head. 'Just yourselves and a sense of fun.'

'We can do that.'

Cari sipped at her espresso before darting a glance at her brother, a mischievous glance that had Lola bracing for the next incoming missile.

'Will you be popping down to Mount Macedon while we're there?'

To his credit, Chase didn't miss a beat. 'Depends on my work schedule but I'd like to drop by, make sure you and the chooks aren't tearing the place apart.'

'Riiight.'

How Cari managed to instil so much innuendo into that one word she'd never know, so Lola rushed in again.

'I'll be commuting daily, though I've cleared the possibility of staying over two nights with Chase.'

'Commute?' Cari's shriek intimated she equated commuting the hour between Melbourne and Mount Macedon with a daily trip to the moon.

Jabbing a finger at her brother, Cari said, 'Tell her she can't do that. She'll be exhausted driving back at the end of a day, then having to get up and do it all over again the next.'

Before Chase could open his mouth to respond, Cari glared at her. 'It's ludicrous. You're staying. I take it you have someone running the shop while you're doing this?'

'Of course but—'

'Then it's settled. Right, Chase?'

Sending her a quick shrug and an apologetic wink, Chase nodded.

'You're the boss, sis.'

'And don't either of you forget it.'

With an emphatic nod and a self-satisfied smirk, Cari resumed drinking her espresso as if nothing had happened, as if she hadn't just railroaded them.

What was it with these Etheridges?

First Chase had steamrollered her into accepting this job, now Cari.

It was going to be some week.

CHAPTER SIX

Two weeks later Lola hefted the last case into the back of the van and collapsed against the tailgate alongside Imogen.

'I must be insane for agreeing to do this,' she muttered, wiping the perspiration from her brow while stretching out her right calf which had cramped after countless trips between Go Retro and the back alley where they'd filled the van to capacity.

'Think of the publicity.' Imogen moaned as she locked fingers, stretched forward and rolled her neck. 'And the massive bonus you're going to pay me for lugging all these bloody boxes out here.'

'I'll think about it.' Lola smiled, a smile that soon faded as she glanced over her shoulder at the floor to roof boxes. 'Guess the logistics of this escaped me in the excitement of Chase's whopping great fee.'

'I wonder if that's the only whopping great thing Chase has—'

'Isn't it time you locked up and headed home?'

The last thing she needed was more of Immy's teasing. She'd bombarded her the entire afternoon as they'd closed up shop to organise the props for the hen's party, firing constant questions at her about her meeting with

Chase—she'd told her friend nothing—and when that didn't work, resorting to childish teasing interspersed with ribald insinuations.

As if she wasn't nervous enough about the coming week.

Imogen sniggered and glanced at her watch. 'Is it that time already? Time for you to hit the road and go shack up with your billionaire.'

'This isn't a romance novel,' Lola said, straightening and brushing off her dusty butt.

She had no intention of shacking up with anyone in the near future, especially not a career-driven charmer who wouldn't know a white picket fence if he drove into one.

When she *shacked up* it would be with Mr Right, not Mr Flirt-Like-Crazy-And-Hope-For-The-Best.

She'd once thought Bodey was shacking up material; until their relationship had taken the next step and he'd bolted quicker than her sister at the sight of a pavlova.

'Maybe you should read a few. Couldn't hurt.'

She could've ignored Imogen's sly sideways glance but knew it'd be useless. Her friend would expound her latest theory anyway.

With a resigned sigh, she perched on the tailgate again.

'And why should I read those romance novels you have your nose constantly buried in?'

Imogen held up her hand. 'Because they're great entertainment.'

She ticked off the first finger. 'Because they're great escapism.'

Another finger bent down. 'Because they give you

great pointers to handle your very own billionaire when he comes along.'

Lola opened her mouth to protest she didn't have her very own billionaire but Imogen shushed her.

The last finger bent. 'And because they get you in the mood, particularly the really steamy ones. Some of those scenes…'

Imogen fanned herself while Lola tried to ignore her friend's salient arguments in favour of romance novels.

Since when had she read anything other than business journals anyway? She never had time for fun stuff any more. Even her weekend trips scouring the markets and auction houses had as much to do with work as pleasure.

She loved Go Retro and everything it stood for but it had become her life these days and, while she adored every inch of her dream come true, she sacrificed a lot to get it off the ground.

And keep it going. Which was why she'd loaded her van and would soon take off for Mount Macedon and spend a week in a guy's house—a guy who might or might not pop in—but the thought alone was enough to have her on tenterhooks the entire time.

The money carving a huge chunk off her mortgage was a major incentive but she'd be lying if she didn't admit a shiver of excitement at the thought of seeing Chase again.

'I've sold you, haven't I?'

Imogen snapped her fingers. 'I can see that twinkle in your eye. Wait here.'

Before she could protest, Immy had shot back into

Go Retro, no doubt to rummage through her massive handbag for the stack of novels she had on the go all at once.

Grinning at her friend's exuberance, and a romantic streak no amount of lousy dates or failed relationships could dim, she hopped off the tailgate and slammed it shut, securing the locks.

She could hit the road before Imogen returned but she wouldn't put it past her single-minded friend to follow her all the way to Mount Macedon just to ply her with romance novels, then stick around to ply Chase with questions about the imaginary relationship she'd built up in her head.

Snagging the keys, she swung up into the van and started the engine. At the sound, Imogen shot out of the back door and ran to the van, shoving a mini stack of novels through the window.

'Here, take these.' She winked. 'You can thank me later.'

Shaking her head, Lola glanced at the covers. *Hot Nights with a Playboy. Big-Shot Bachelor. The Boss's Bedroom Agenda. Purchased for Pleasure,* the titles punctuated by provocative pictures of women in clinches with gorgeous men.

Half their luck.

An image popped unbidden into her mind, a memory fragment of Chase kissing the back of her hand, his lips curving into a sexy smile, his incredibly blue eyes dark with promise...and in that fleeting instant, she wished she could believe she did fascinate him.

Imogen tapped the top cover—*Two-Week Mistress.* 'Change the title to One-Week and it could be you.'

Lola rolled her eyes as Imogen giggled. 'Trust me, read those and you won't put a foot wrong with your Chase.' Immy's eyes glinted with mischief. 'Then when you get back I'll lend you some more appropriate titles, along the lines of *The Billionaire's Baby*.'

Unable to do anything but laugh at her friend's antics, she pointed to her pride and joy.

'Take good care of the place.'

'Shall do.'

Imogen saluted and tapped the van's bonnet. 'And you take good care of our place's reputation. Give 'em a hen's party to remember.'

As she put the van into gear and eased off on the clutch to protect the precious cargo in the back, Imogen cupped her hands around her mouth and yelled, 'As for your reputation, cut loose. Take a leaf out of Ariel's story and get the hero naked. She's the heroine in *Big-Shot Bachelor—*'

Lola gunned the engine and drove off, effectively cutting off any more of Imogen's relationship wisdom.

She could take care of her own love life, thank you very much.

What little there was of it.

Casting a quick look at the pile of novels on the front seat beside her, seeing the ecstatic expression on the heroine's face made her wonder if maybe, just maybe, there was something to Imogen's prescription for romance after all.

Chase thrived on a challenge. He'd relished working his butt off at the roughest high school in North Melbourne to gain a good entry score for university, he'd studied hard at uni to get an honours degree in economics and he'd worked harder and longer than anyone in the entertainment business to launch Dazzle then keep it at the top.

He'd procured international stars to perform at local millionaires' parties, he'd MC'd top line charity balls, he'd organised bands and caterers and dancers for major AFL functions, rising to each and every challenge.

But nothing in his busy life challenged him as much as facing his mother.

With a resigned sigh he shoved his smartphone back in his jacket after signing off on another A-list shindig and headed up the familiar path winding through Melbourne University's sprawling campus.

He knew this path well, had traipsed it many times growing up. It had been the only time he ever got to see his parents, if he made the trek here after school.

Initially, he'd found their snatched hour together between lectures fun. How many other kids got to have picnic dinners with their parents every evening? And usually at a different location: the main lawns, outside the library, on a park bench.

It had been exciting, like having a new adventure every day. But it grew tiring after a while, having to drag a tired Cari home by himself on public transport, battling peak hour commuters on a tram, before getting her settled for bed then starting on his homework.

As he grew older and his parents' work commitments increased the higher up the university faculty ladder they climbed, the dinner picnics dwindled as his resentment built. Why couldn't he have parents who came home at a reasonable hour, parents who helped with homework,

parents who cared more about their kids than their precious bloody jobs?

Not that those picnics had been anything special.
Looking back, those snatched hours were probably his
folks' way of paying lip service to spending time with
their kids. A way to assuage their guilt at being absentee
parents? A way to indoctrinate them into the uni life at
a young age? A way to soothe their disappointment that
their kids weren't born child geniuses?

He'd wondered over the years at why they'd ever decided to become parents in the first place but had come
to no conclusions. For a while, he'd wondered if they'd
had kids as some kind of sociological experiment and
when he and Cari couldn't hold a proper conversation
by the age of five they were deemed not important.

Not that he'd noticed the lack of affection at the
start. They had nannies to provide the basics, until he
was old enough to fend for himself and then he'd taken
over as Cari's carer. That was when the resentment had
kicked in and he'd been pondering their motivation ever
since.

Why have kids if you didn't give a toss about
them?

Not that they were deliberately mean or nasty; they
just weren't *there*. Cari's first ballet concert, his first
high school debate, Cari's debutante ball, his graduation;
they'd been absent for it all and despite a continuing
apathy over the years he couldn't help but wish they'd
acknowledge how far their kids had come, just once.

He'd practically raised Cari and now, when their mum
should be involved in wedding stuff, once again it was
left to him to take on the parental role.

Trying to stem his rising animosity, he wound his way through students coming the other way, dodging hefty backpacks and book-laden arms.

Had he ever been as carefree as some of these kids looked? Wide smiles, clear eyes, filled with hope and expectation and love for life?

It annoyed him, to think he'd never had a chance to be so blithe and, as he neared the English faculty building, the loss of his childhood stung as much as his parents' indifference.

Trudging up the stairs, he entered the centuries old sandstone building and turned right, heading down the end of a long corridor to the last door on the left.

Ridiculous that he hovered, bracing himself, when he'd walked into hostile meetings many times before.

Increasingly grim at having to do this, he knocked twice before entering, knowing from experience he'd be waiting outside all day if he expected a 'come in'.

When English professor Belinda Etheridge was in her office stampeding elephants couldn't distract her from whatever dissertation she was working on. He knew, boy, did he know.

As always, she didn't look up from the paper she was poring over, her hair a messy greying bun perched on top of her head and stuck with a pen, her hippy clothes straight off the rack from the local second-hand shop.

He cleared his throat to the usual response—nothing—and striding across the small office, he tapped her on the shoulder.

'What—who—oh, it's you, Chase,' she said, flashing a quick smile before her gaze was already drifting back to her paper.

'Hey, Mum.'

He waited, playing this stupid game, waiting to see how long she'd take to respond. Futile, maybe. Childish, definitely, but it really irked to stand here and wait for his own mother to finish whatever was more important than him today to finally acknowledge him.

'Just give me a minute to wrap this up—'

'Sorry, don't have the time today.'

And he didn't; didn't have time for this any longer. He was here for one reason and one reason only: Cari.

'You know Cari's getting married in a few weeks?'

He could've sworn her shoulders stiffened before she pushed back from her desk at a snail's pace, making a great show of folding her arms and frowning, as if he'd interrupted research on finding a cancer cure.

'Yes, I vaguely remember something about it.'

Familiar fury shot through him but he damped it. He'd do the right thing and then he was out of here.

'I'm throwing a hen's party for her. It involves a dinner next Friday night. If you're free, you're welcome to come.'

Her frown deepened. 'Next Friday? Let me see…I don't think…hang on…'

While she rummaged through the mess on her desk for her elusive diary, the irony of the situation wasn't lost on him. Shouldn't it be a mother's role to organise this kind of thing in lieu of bridesmaids? Shouldn't Belinda be throwing Cari a dinner/shower/hen's night? Shouldn't she at least *show* some excitement that her only daughter was getting hitched?

Then again, she'd barely acknowledged her only

daughter existed growing up, why the hell should she change now?

'Friday night, you said?'

She flipped diary pages, landed on one and ran her finger down a full page. 'No, sorry, faculty meeting.'

He gritted his teeth at her blasé response, her almost relieved tone.

How on earth had this woman taken time out from her busy schedule to have one child, let alone two?

Giving it one last shot for Cari's sake, he asked, 'You can't change it?'

Or, better yet, miss it for once in your selfish life?

She shook her head before he'd barely finished asking the question.

'Too important. I'll catch up with Cari another time.'

He could've done what he'd always done: nodded, mumbled some lame-assed response and left before his resentment spilled out in a gush of temper.

Not this time.

'Bull.'

Her mouth dropped open before quickly snapping shut in a thin, unimpressed line. 'Watch your manners, son.'

'Son? *Son?*'

He laughed, a harsh sound with a maniacal edge. 'That's rich, coming from you.'

Her eyes narrowed before she swivelled away on her ergonomic chair, the only modern touch in the office.

'I haven't got time for this.'

'You never have time for anything unless it's your precious bloody job!' he shouted, furious with himself for losing control but needing to rattle her enough to get some kind of reaction other than the years of indifference he and Cari had put up with.

'Don't you get it? Your only daughter is getting married and rather than celebrating with her you'd prefer to be holed up in this mausoleum on a Friday night with a bunch of old cronies. It's ludicrous.'

She didn't turn around to face him but he saw his accusations strike home in every rigid muscle of her neck, in her erect posture.

'To you, maybe. But it's important to me.'

Dragging a hand through his hair, he shook his head. Why was he wasting his time? Nothing he said would ever get through to her.

'That's just it, isn't it, Mum? It's all about you. It's always been all about you and stuff your kids.'

He held his breath, hoping the truth he'd finally flung at her would get a reaction, hoping she'd give him some small indication she really did care despite her years of indifference.

As the taut silence stretched, he knew what he was hoping to hear was on a par with the wish he'd had as a six-year-old—that Santa was real.

He spun on his heel in disgust and headed for the door, his hand on the handle when she said, 'We're coming to the wedding. We had a class graduation on but chose to see Cari get married instead.'

The small part of him, quashed deep down inside that still yearned for her attention, was grateful for that at least.

But the rest of him, bristling with resentment and

rage and disappointment, wanted to yell, *It should've been no contest!* as he opened the door.

'Glad you can take time out from your *inflexible* schedule,' he spat out before he slammed it behind him.

CHAPTER SEVEN

LOLA had grown up in a large house, a sprawling Queenslander with cool white shutters, a veranda circling the house and enough rooms so she didn't have to run into her narcissistic mum and sister too often, which had suited her just fine.

Thanks to Shareen's fame and the money her mum invested, they'd lived comfortably. But as she drove up the sweeping driveway towards Chase's Mount Macedon hideaway and caught a glimpse of a huge sandstone mansion tucked between the towering gums *living comfortably* took on a whole new meaning.

As the van rounded the final bend, her mouth dropped open at the sheer size of the place. The front of the architect designed house lay across half an acre, its creamy splendour highlighted against a backdrop of the muted green Aussie bush. Its huge wooden-framed windows ran the length of the house, ensuring stunning views from every room and, as the van bounced over a pothole and she over-corrected, she wondered what would keep a man shut away in that clinical penthouse when he could live surrounded by all this beauty.

Towering eucalypts framed a garden filled with her favourite natives, bottle brushes and wattles, while a carefully maintained Japanese garden could be seen tucked off to one side, rich with bonsai and white pebbles and lanterns.

Then again, from what she'd seen of Chase Etheridge, a go-getting over-achiever would rarely take time out to smell the banksias. Yet to leave this place vacant…

Shaking her head, she pulled up near the back door, surprised when it flew open and Cari bounded out, a poster girl for casual chic in her designer navy velour leisure suit, the nautical scarf tied around her head like a bandanna another touch of vintage.

She liked that about the businesswoman, how she found ways to add a little bit of retro to her modern wardrobe.

'Hey, Lola, you found the place okay?'

She nodded, slipped out of the driver's seat and unkinked her back.

'Yeah, Chase's instructions were spot on.'

Cari's eyes twinkled. 'How is my brother?'

Lola shrugged, hoping a blush wouldn't undermine the professional image she'd hoped to maintain this next week. 'I wouldn't know, haven't seen him.'

'Really?'

Cari's mouth drooped in disappointment and Lola smothered a laugh. What would Chase think of his sister adding matchmaker to her CV?

'I could've sworn he has a thing for you. Who knows, maybe he'll pop down here this week—'

'Is there anyone to give me a hand unloading?'

Lola didn't want to think about Chase popping in, not when she had a job to do. As for him having a thing for her, of course he was fascinated by her. She wore big boofy skirts and big hair and big accessories, the complete opposite of the sleek, slinky women he mixed with.

'I'll help.'

'No, you're the guest of honour—'

'I'm also the only one here at the moment. Marta, the housekeeper, has been given the week off so you can have your run of the place and the rest of the girls aren't arriving until this afternoon.'

Cari flexed her muscles. 'So let's start unpacking.'

Feeling guilty at taking Chase's money and getting the hen to help her unload, she unlocked the back of the van with reluctance, unprepared for a loud ear-splitting squeal of delight as Cari caught sight of the first travel trunk.

'Oh, my goodness! Where did you get this?'

Buoyed by a fellow vintage groupie, Lola tapped the top of the trunk. 'An old steamer in England was auctioning off its contents and they had a stack of these old trunks. Cool, huh?'

'Wow! I can't wait to see what's inside them.'

Cari's eyes sparkled with enthusiasm, her expression rapt, and Lola knew that whatever she dished up for the bride-to-be this week she'd be happy.

It made her job a heck of a lot easier when the people she ran parties for liked her stuff and while she'd had girls gush before she'd never met someone quite on her wavelength like Cari.

Funnily enough, Cari almost intrigued her as much as Chase. The slick corporate lawyer she'd seen stride into Chase's office when they'd first met was nothing like this bright-eyed, gushing vintage devotee.

Was Chase like that too? All slick and corporate on the outside but with underlying depths she couldn't imagine?

Cari hoisted the first box. 'Come on, let's get a move on. I want to start playing.'

Lola smiled and tsked-tsked as she slid two boxes into her arms and followed Cari towards the house. 'Most of this stuff is supposed to be a surprise so you'll have to wait.'

'What, no preview?'

Chuckling at Cari's outrage, she juggled the boxes to get a better grip as they stepped up into the house. 'Well, maybe I'll let you rifle through one box.'

'That's all?'

'Take it or leave it.'

Smiling, Cari led her into a big, airy mud room, big enough to hold all her trunks and boxes and then some. 'Just my luck, I get the tough party hostess.'

Amazed at how easily they were getting along, Lola dumped her boxes where Cari pointed.

'I'm also the hostess with the mostest so you're extremely lucky.'

'Not as lucky as I'm hoping my brother's going to get.'

With a wink, Cari ducked back outside and headed towards the van, leaving Lola wondering what it was about the Etheridge siblings that had her so enthralled.

She never took to people quickly, never had, probably born of years of being self-conscious about her weight and appearance next to the other gene-blessed females in her family.

Shy, reserved, bookish, all terms she'd grown up with

and even when she'd reinvented herself she hadn't lost her reservations. If anything, having people suddenly pay her attention because of how she looked made her more wary.

She'd taken a while to warm up to Imogen, her closest friend these days, so the speed at which she'd bonded with Cari left her reeling.

As for her blossoming crush on Chase and how fast he had her under his spell… She stubbed her toe on the corner of a box, cursing the man with the power to distract her, bamboozle her and confound her.

After seeing his mother last night, Chase had headed back to the office and pulled an all-nighter.

He'd needed to work off his frustration, to focus on something solid and real and tangible, something he understood, and that definitely wasn't his mother.

Grabbing a two-hour nap at the office, followed by a shower, shave and double shot espresso, should've had him awake and ready to go. It wasn't as if he hadn't pulled all-nighters before.

But this morning was different and as his distracted gaze drifted to the time on the bottom right hand corner of his PC screen for the umpteenth time, he knew he was kidding himself.

Throwing himself into work last night may have worked where his mum was concerned but this morning, knowing Lola was at his house, preparing for the week ahead, made working impossible.

Gritting his teeth, he pulled up the latest projections figures for the Spring Racing Carnival's gala ball, yet another feather in Dazzle's impressive cap.

The figures danced before his eyes and he couldn't concentrate on the spreadsheet for more than thirty seconds. He pushed away from his desk and stood, bracing himself against the window as he stared at Melbourne's CBD sprawled out before him thirty floors below.

He loved this view, usually found solace in the height, seemingly perched on top of the world, right where he wanted to be. And so far removed from his parents' academia to make him feel vindicated about every choice he'd ever made.

Being this high, being on top in his business, made him feel like a king. He worked hard, he partied hard yet the longer he stood here and surveyed the city that made his blood fizz with opportunity he couldn't ignore the slight hollowness that insisted there was more to life than this.

Dragging a hand through his hair he turned away from the million dollar view and glanced at his watch. Plenty of time to put in a solid day's work and stop dwelling on the inevitable empty feeling and the niggling yearning for one iota of acknowledgement meeting with his folks always dragged up.

Was that the only reason he felt this edgy?

No, he wouldn't think about Lola, wouldn't wonder what she was doing in his house, wouldn't contemplate driving up there to visit and oversee proceedings.

He'd hired Lola to do a job. She was a professional, she'd handle it without his interference.

But it was his house; he knew every nook and cranny. What if she needed a hand?

The fact he had a very competent housekeeper flashed

through his head for a second before he remembered Cari had insisted he gave Marta the week off.

Besides, Cari was his sister, his only sibling, and he'd gone to all this trouble to organise a hen's party she wouldn't forget. Only seemed right he popped down there and made sure everything was going smoothly.

Cursing himself for being a sad case, he pulled his laptop closer and concentrated on work. Having his voice of reason mentally slug it out with his impulsive side was a waste of time. All the self-justifying arguments in the world wouldn't drive him to abandon his work for the day and head down to that hen's party.

No way.

Four hours later, in this kind of mood, the last thing Chase should be doing was driving out to Mount Macedon.

He avoided the place at the best of times, its welcoming homeliness a reminder of what he didn't have and never would.

Living in outer suburbia with the requisite two point five kids, golden Labrador and claustrophobic family commitments wasn't for him. He'd decided that a long time ago when his parents had the expected family but ignored them anyway.

So why buy the house in the first place?

He'd deliberately ignored that question whenever it popped into his subconscious, citing all kinds of logical reasons why he'd bought the sprawling family home two years ago. A good investment. An opportunity to capitalise when the housing market was good. A sound business decision.

All very acceptable reasons for purchasing a home he rarely visited but deep down, in those rare times he allowed himself to stop running on overdrive, he acknowledged the whispered truth.

That his Mount Macedon mansion represented what he'd wanted his whole life: a real home.

Turning up the surround sound stereo in his Jag to drown out his annoying thoughts, he exited the freeway, trying to ignore his mounting anticipation.

If he didn't know any better, he'd almost say he was looking forward to crashing this hen's party.

Crazy, as seeing Cari and her ditzy friends play dress up didn't hold the slightest bit of interest. But seeing Lola Lombard again did and he allowed himself the luxury of a self-satisfied grin as he imagined her reaction when he rocked up.

She wouldn't be happy.

She'd purse those ruby-red lips in disapproval, would pout and frown all she liked but he knew the truth: she too felt the buzz between them.

And that was what had ultimately drawn him here.

He wanted to rid his mind of his mother's callous indifference, of the mountain of work waiting for him, and do something guaranteed to take his mind off everything. Flirting with Lola was it.

Feeling like a ton weight had been lifted off his shoulders since he'd left Melbourne, he turned into his drive, the house giving him a familiar thrill as he caught his first glimpse. The thrill was tinged with a hint of bittersweet longing, a yearning for the family life he couldn't risk having.

Annoyed at the momentary blight on his anticipation,

he swerved to a stop near the back door, right next to a decrepit lemon-yellow van with flowers stencilled down the side.

The florists in town wouldn't drive something so utterly appalling, which meant the death trap on wheels could only belong to one person.

As he stepped from the car and gave the van a closer inspection—the rust speckles, the dented bumpers, the unlockable doors—he knew Lola was taking her love of old stuff to extremes.

The fact she'd made it here in one piece in that thing was a miracle and, as he barged towards the back door, it hit him why he was so mad.

He cared. Cared about what she drove, cared about her safety, cared too much full stop for a woman he was irrationally, increasingly attracted to.

When he reached the veranda he stopped and dragged in several deep breaths. No point barging in all wound up about something that wasn't his business. What she drove, where she drove it, was entirely up to her and taking out his lingering gripes against his mum from last night on her wouldn't achieve anything bar push her away.

And that was one thing he certainly didn't want. Now he was here he intended on getting closer to Lola Lombard—a lot closer.

Somewhat calmer, he strode into the kitchen; and came to an abrupt stop.

Lola stood at the stove wearing a ridiculous pink frilly apron, stirring something that smelled suspiciously like Beef Stroganoff, a dish he'd cooked too many times as a kid.

Having her in his kitchen, looking like the good little housewife waiting for a devoted hubby to come home, left him feeling hollow.

This was exactly why he never came here; it reminded him too much of what he'd never had, how much he resented it.

Not that he'd expected his mum to slave over a hot stove and wait for his dad to walk in the door—far from it—but it was the whole concept of family, of warmth, of cosiness, that he'd craved growing up.

Just once he would've liked to come home to this scene—just once. But he'd never had a home-cooked meal, not one he hadn't made himself, and as for a sit down family dinner? Try never.

Lola looked up at that moment, her eyes initially widening in surprise before lighting with pleasure, eradicating his bad memories in an instant.

'Let me guess. Cari coerced you into cooking her favourite.'

She smiled and swiped her hands down the front of her apron. 'The other girls aren't arriving till tomorrow morning now and we got to talking about dinner and she mentioned you used to whip up a mean Stroganoff so I offered...'

She trailed off, her eyelashes giving a nervous flutter as he stepped close enough to haul her into his arms.

'That's nice,' he said, his fingers toying with the apron strings, his gaze never leaving hers, picking up every flicker of emotion—fear, nervousness, excitement—and it was the last that urged him to throw caution and close the small gap between them.

'But right now I'm not interested in my sister's dinner.'

He slid a hand around her waist, rested it in the small of her back and tugged her forward until her breasts brushed his chest and he bit back a groan.

'I'm far more interested in discovering if there's anything you can't do.'

Her lips parted but he didn't give her a chance to respond, covering her mouth with his in a searing kiss guaranteed to keep him up at night.

She resisted for less than a second, her lips softening, responding, before she really let go and clutched at his lapels, kissing him back with a ferocity that stunned him.

He had no idea how long they stood there, locked in an embrace neither wanted to end, savouring long, hot kisses that went on for ever but if the stove hadn't given a startling hiss he seriously doubted whether he would've been able to stop.

'Damn,' she muttered, grabbing a ladle and giving the fettuccine a furious stir, and he had no idea if she was mad at the water bubbling over onto the pristine stainless steel stove or at him for that mind-blowing kiss.

'Cari's in the study looking at bridal magazines,' she said, her tone dismissive, but she couldn't hide her ragged breathing or the blush staining her cheeks.

'Maybe I didn't come out all this way to see Cari?'

Her shoulders stiffened before she resumed her vigorous stirring.

'Of course you did. What other reason—'

'I like you, Lola. So stop pretending that sensational

kiss didn't happen and admit you feel this zing as much as I do.'

Her hand holding the ladle trembled ever so slightly before she snatched it out of the boiling water and stuck it in a holder.

Folding her arms in a typical hands-off posture, she reluctantly met his gaze.

'You hired me to do a job and I intend to do it to the best of my ability. I can't afford distractions.'

'Is that all I am to you?'

His gaze drifted to her sensual lips, to their luscious ruby sheen that hadn't budged despite their serious lip locking as he briefly wondered what she'd look like without the war paint.

Her lips compressed into a thin red slash. 'Fine, you want me to say we share a spark? We do. But come on, Chase, you've shared enough sparks with women across Melbourne to create your own bonfire.'

He laughed, as delighted by her sense of humour as the rest of her.

'I'm not a monk. But I date for convenience rather than any grand passion. How about you?'

He'd caught her off guard with his bluntness, her instant flare of panic replaced by an emotion he didn't expect: sadness.

She shrugged, sending a longing glance at the stove as if she'd rather get back to it.

'I don't have much time to date these days. Go Retro takes up all my time.'

'That's plain wrong.' He shook his head and captured her chin when she tried to look away again. 'A beautiful woman like you should be wined and dined. You should be dancing and clubbing and cutting a swathe through Melbourne.'

The corners of her mouth twitched before she swatted away his hand.

'If I had more downtime I'd spend it at an art exhibition or a poetry reading or book launches.'

Disappointed by her staid choices, he silently chastised himself for caring, again. This was nothing more than a flirtation to him, a pleasant way to pass the time, a nice distraction from the increasing edginess that pervaded everything he did lately.

He'd initially blamed it on worry at Cari heading down the matrimonial path, then later on a few business deals that had almost gone south.

But walking into this kitchen, seeing Lola again, blew his lame excuses sky high.

The reason behind his restlessness these days was a general dissatisfaction that no matter how much money he made or how many condos he invested in or how many A-list parties he attended, there was more to life.

'I can see how riveting you'd find my social life.'

She turned back to the stove, any inroads into establishing camaraderie banished by his obvious disdain for anything remotely arty.

'It's good having different interests. Opposites attracting and all that?'

With an annoyed huff that made her lips pout deliciously, she stuck her hands on her hips and stared him down. 'You're a flirt; I get it. But I've got more important things to do, if you don't mind?'

Ducking down to her ear, he murmured, 'Ah, but I do mind.'

Her exasperated curse was tempered by an underlying hint of amusement. 'Are you staying for dinner?'

'Sweetheart, I'm staying for the week.'

With that parting shot that shocked him as much as it did her, he headed for the study, leaving a delightfully flustered woman gaping after him.

CHAPTER EIGHT

LOLA shoved the pasta around her plate with a fork, occasionally making a show of guiding a small piece of beef into her mouth but tasting nothing.

Sitting here with Cari and Chase, listening to their easy banter, was all a bit surreal. She'd expected to be working her butt off the moment she arrived, not enjoying a casual dinner with two people she could easily see herself being friends with.

The heat of Chase's gaze landed on her and she choked on the next mouthful.

Friends? Not a hope in hell.

The memory of that sizzling kiss in the kitchen had her reaching for a glass of water and downing the lot. It did little to cool her, her body on perpetual fire since he'd annihilated all her carefully prepared, well-rehearsed reasons why this week couldn't be more than work.

She hadn't expected him to turn up but on the drive here she'd gone through many reasons to keep him at arm's length if he did.

They were opposites in every way.

He was looking for a good time in a short time; she wanted the best time for ever.

He thrived on mod cons; she knew every shoe buckle circa nineteen fifty but wouldn't know a smartphone from an iPad.

All very sane, logical reasons and she'd been determined to keep things between them strictly business if he did show his face.

Well, she could kiss her logic goodbye now, just like she'd kissed him without restraint.

Lord, she'd come apart the moment his lips touched hers, her body lighting up like a firecracker on New Year's Eve.

How long since she'd been kissed like that?

One word echoed through her head…*never*…and she risked a quick glance at the guy who'd rocked her world.

While Cari droned on about some stunt Hugh had pulled, Chase nodded and 'ah-ha'd in all the right places, but his gaze was firmly fixed on her.

She gulped, desperate to ease the tightness in her throat, for if either of them asked her anything her answer would come out an embarrassing squeak.

Sensing her discomfort, he smiled and raised his Shiraz in her direction, taunting her to what? Admit to this annoying, unavoidable attraction between them? Give in to whatever game he wanted to play?

Not likely but the longer he stared at her with those intense blue eyes, the harder it was to stay focused on her resolve to concentrate on work.

'What do you think, Lola?'

Cursing the man who'd distracted her to the point of tuning out of the conversation completely, she swung her gaze to Cari, wondering how she could fluff an answer to whatever question she'd asked.

Putting down his fork, Chase steepled his fingers together, his smug grin making her itch to dump the Stroganoff in his lap.

'Yes, tell us, Lola, we'd love to hear your opinion on my multitasking skills.'

Okay, so he'd thrown her a lifeline and saved her from mortification. Didn't mean she had to let him off easy.

Tapping her chin, she pretended to think. 'Considering you could barely function for two minutes when I confiscated your phone in my shop, I'd say you're not doing so great.'

Cari's mouth dropped open. 'You touched his precious smartphone?' Letting out a loud hoot, she clapped her hands. 'Never thought I'd see the day.'

Chase's quick glance in his sister's direction should've warned her that what came next wouldn't be good.

Chuckling, Cari punched Chase on the arm. 'Lola, if this guy let you touch his phone, you're practically engaged.'

Inwardly cringing, Lola glanced at Chase, expecting to laugh off his sister's exuberant teasing with his help. She expected him to make light of it, crack a joke, fire back a quip.

What she didn't expect was the horrified expression turning his face stony. And that was when her little fantasy bubble well and truly popped.

For no matter how much Chase flirted with her, how many times he touched her or charmed her or kissed her, it was all a game to him.

A guy like him would never get serious about a girl like her.

Apparently she wasn't marriage material, not for him.

'More bread?'

Lola all but shoved the basket in Cari's direction; she'd twigged something wasn't right with her brother and was giving him time to compose himself.

'Yeah, thanks.'

Darting a quick glance in Chase's direction then rolling her eyes, Cari resumed conversation as if nothing had happened, glossing over the engagement joke faux pas as if it had never happened.

And while Chase joined in again, a practised socialite at his charming best, the gloss of the evening had worn off.

A long ten minutes later, Lola begged off dessert and made a dash for the safety of her room.

Lola couldn't sleep.

She tried: everything from counting sheep to mentally checking inventory to running through the itinerary for the next week.

Nothing worked. Every time she closed her eyes all she could see was Chase's deep blue eyes, his sexy smile, his intent expression the second before he'd kissed her… followed by his appalled expression at the thought of being engaged to her.

That was what haunted her the most, the fact he could flirt and charm and kiss her, but the slightest hint of anything more serious sent him scuttling.

Not that she'd consider marrying him for a moment—

she didn't believe in his opposites attracting hoo-ha—but if he balked at a joke about it, what did he really think of her?

A nice little distraction for the week? A bit of fun? Someone he could toy with before moving on to his next infatuation?

Ha! As if she'd ever consider marrying someone like him. He'd have to crawl through the bush over tiger snakes and wild boars and feral dogs for her to even think about it, and then she'd still say no.

With a frustrated groan she rolled out of bed, snagged her dressing gown off the end of the bed and shrugged into it. A nice cup of chamomile tea might take the edge off her insomnia. Though, as she padded down the hallway in the darkness, her bare feet thankfully silent on the marble polished floors, she realised her foolishness.

Cari had given her a quick rundown of the kitchen earlier but where the heck would she find chamomile tea?

She daredn't turn on the lights for the last thing she needed was Chase coming to investigate a midnight marauder in the kitchen.

Feeling her way through the monstrous stainless steel and granite kitchen, she flicked on the small light on the range hood over the stove, casting enough light into the kitchen but not enough to wake snoozing charmers—hopefully.

Rifling through the well-stocked pantry, she spied a huge range of teas on the middle shelf and grabbing the chamomile she dumped a bag into a mug while waiting for the kettle to boil.

How many times had she done this as a teenager—sneaking into the kitchen in the dead of night while the rest of her perfectly proportioned family slept?

Contrary to their beliefs, she'd never gorged on chocolates or cakes or chips. She'd just preferred having the kitchen to herself so she could sit down with a mug of cocoa and a piece of toast in peace without having her plate scrutinised.

She'd hated that, hated the constant calorie counting and portion cutting at every meal just so her mum could stay slim and her sister wouldn't gain a pound before her next fashion show.

They'd never believed she didn't eat junk food on the sly, always glaring suspiciously when she ate the same rabbit food as them but continued to weigh the equivalent of both of them combined.

How many times had she stared at herself in the mirror, loathing her curves, wondering why she looked like an elephant stuck between two gazelles?

Other people had thought the same: she'd seen it in their critical stares, their barely concealed distaste as they'd fawned over her mum and Shareen, deeming her not worth a second glance when their judgemental glances flicked over her.

Ironic, when she'd finally grown into her own body, had shed the puppy fat naturally and embraced her curves with clothes and styles that suited her rather than squeezing into outfits deemed worthy by her mum but that did nothing for her figure, those same people had wanted to know who the newest Lombard female was.

Flicking off the kettle before it could whistle, she poured boiling water in her cup and dunked the tea bag a few times, the familiar action soothing. Herbal tea had been the only fad of her mum's she'd actually embraced and hoping it did the trick tonight she cradled the mug in her hands and headed for the lounge room.

Curling up with her chamomile in a suede recliner, staring out at the beautiful bushland bathed in moonlight through the floor to ceiling windows, would hopefully calm her into sleep.

As she neared the lounge she heard voices coming from the study, the soft spill of light illuminating the hallway in a gentle glow.

Damn, she needed to pass the study to get to the lounge. The smart thing to do would be head back to the safety of her bedroom but curiosity urged her forward. Besides, the study door was mainly closed. She could tiptoe past without interrupting whoever was burning the midnight oil.

However, as she edged past the door, she stopped, captured by the sight of Chase sitting behind another monstrous glass desk, his crisp white business shirt unbuttoned, sleeves rolled up to the elbows, his fingers flying over a laptop keyboard while he issued instructions into a Dictaphone.

He barely drew breath, barking out orders while typing simultaneously, his frantic work pace in the middle of the night startling.

Was this the norm for him? She'd thought he was a workaholic but not taking the time to change out of his business suit, stuck in his study at all hours when he'd escaped the city and had this beautiful house to relax in?

She didn't get it. Sure, Go Retro was her life but

she liked nothing better than chilling out over a skinny
latte at her favourite St Kilda café or strolling along the
boardwalk at Port Melbourne or her favourite, trawling
the markets on lazy Sunday afternoons.

What drove a guy like Chase?

He had money to burn, probably didn't have to work
these manic hours yet here he was holed up in the early
hours of the morning, pushing himself while the rest of
the world slumbered.

Well, most of the world and as she gripped her mug
tighter and took a step forward, he glanced up, sensing
her presence.

Cursing her curiosity for landing her in this predica-
ment, she raised her mug in his direction. 'Just having
a late night cuppa. I'll leave you to it.'

'Stay.'

He stood, moved around the desk towards her and
she held her breath, the weariness shadowing his eyes
making her yearn to reach out and erase the dark circles
testifying to his long hours.

'Please.'

His soft plea persuaded her as much as his puzzlingly
bleak expression and she warily nodded, entering the
study while wishing she had something more appropriate on. Slinky satin might make her feel womanly and
empowered, two things she'd craved to be her entire
life, but holed up in a study with a man she couldn't stop
thinking about made her acutely aware of the purple
satin sliding across her breasts and hips.

Wishing she could tighten the sash around her waist
without upending her cuppa, she sidled towards an

armchair near the open fire, as far away from the next closest chair as possible.

'Couldn't sleep?'

'Yeah, going over the plans for the next week in my head.'

He smiled and her heart squirmed. 'Another workaholic by the sounds of it.'

She glanced at her watch and raised an eyebrow. 'You should know. Do you usually work this late?'

Circumspection settled over his face. 'Depends.'

'On?'

'Whether I need to be distracted from other things.'

The smart thing to do would be sip her chamomile tea and not ask what he needed to be distracted from. But she didn't like the awkward silence stretching taut between them and the longer it continued the more likely she was to blurt something inappropriate.

Taking another fortifying sip of tea, she lowered the mug. 'So what's distracting you?'

The corners of his mouth curved and her heart gave another treacherous twang.

'You really need to ask?'

'Wouldn't have asked if I wasn't interested.'

Pretending to think for a moment, he suddenly snapped his fingers. 'Usually it's an upcoming event or an entertainer that's gone AWOL or a host of unforeseen problems that distracts me from getting on with my job.'

He paused, the intensity behind his stare leaving her in little doubt what he'd say next.

'This time, it's something else entirely.'

He reached out and captured her hand.

'And I'm looking straight at her.'

Heat streaked through her body at his simple touch and when he caressed the back of her hand with his thumb she almost upended the mug of tea sloshing in her other.

Thankfully, he took the mug out of her hands but her relief was short-lived when he sat on the coffee table between their chairs and caught hold of the other one.

'I don't have time for games, Lola. When I want something, I go after it.'

A slow flush crept into her cheeks and she wished she could press her hands against them to cool it.

'So I'm the flavour of the week? It'll pass once I'm out of here.'

She had him.

What could he say? For the truth was a guy like Chase would only be interested in her for the short term before moving onto the next woman who snagged his attention. His horror at Cari's engagement joke was testament to that.

Sure, he seemed a tad smitten now but that would wear off once the uniqueness of their situation did.

She could see him struggling for the right words, the conflict in his eyes: tell her the truth or sweet talk her further.

'Tell me, Chase. Once this *fascination* you profess to have for me wears off, what do you see us being? Friends?'

'Friends is good.'

He grasped at the lifeline she'd thrown him so quickly her head spun.

'But for now I'd rather be more.'

'Are you saying—'

'You're killing me, Lola.'

His eyes drifted to her satin robe, lingering on her cleavage before sweeping up, his heated gaze clashing with her wary one.

'I don't want to sit here and analyse what we are or will be. I don't want to waste our time together.'

He released her hands, his fingertips skating slowly up her arms beneath the satin sleeves, creating havoc with her nerve-endings and her pulse alike.

'I don't want to look back on this week and regret not being upfront about what I want.' He reached her shoulders and gently tugged her forward. 'Can you say the same?'

She couldn't say anything as he drew her towards him, giving her ample opportunity to pull back or say something to put an end to this constant flirtatious merry-go-round they seemed to be spinning on.

Instead, she swallowed every shallow protest and leaned into the inevitable kiss, their lips brushing once, twice, teasing and fleeting, a prelude to what promised to be another cataclysmic kiss.

Her body strained towards him, wanting this with every crazy cell. But then what? She tiptoed around him for the next week, her mind distracted and her body wanting more?

Not good business sense and the thought of what botching this week could potentially mean for Go Retro was enough of a dampener.

She allowed herself the luxury of touching his face, her fingers skimming the stubble along his jaw, drifting upwards to caress his cheekbones, her lips skating across his one last time before she eased away.

'Tell me what you want, Lola.'

I want you screamed through her head, the truth busting to get out.

But she'd spent a lifetime hiding the truth from those closest to her—why change now?

'I want to do a good job this week and taking this flirtation too far is guaranteed to distract me from that.'

Pushing his hands away, she stood, prepared to make another run for it if needed.

'I can't afford to mix business with pleasure. I'm sorry.'

'Not half as sorry as I am,' he murmured, reaching out for her again but she side-stepped and, with a last fleeting glance of regret, she fled.

CHAPTER NINE

LOLA didn't have time to second guess her decision to keep things strictly professional between her and Chase, for the next morning bedlam descended in the form of the four Bs.

She'd initially thought Cari was having her on with her friends' names—Bron, Bryony, Babs and Binnie—but the moment the four poured out of a sleek, low slung convertible, looking like models in a luxury sports car commercial, she knew Cari had been telling the truth.

These four, from the tips of their French manicures to the ends of their pedicured pinkies, were beautiful, bouncy and beyond blonde.

'Oh-oh. Trouble, incoming,' Chase muttered, standing next to her on the front step, watching the girls surround Cari in a flurry of hugs, squeals and laughter.

Surprised at his reserved tone, she said, 'You don't like Cari's friends?'

He shrugged. 'Not my type.'

'Why's that?' The question flew from her lips before she could stop it and she mentally kicked herself for giving away the fact she cared about his answer.

'They're high-maintenance. Women who need to be loved by every man in the room, women who crave

attention more than their next shoe fix, women who
think the way to a man's heart is through his wallet.'

With a smug grin, he added, 'I prefer my women
self-sufficient, warm, enticing, who know the way to a
man's heart is through a decent Beef Stroganoff.'

He sent her a pointed glance and she quickly averted
her gaze, a blush sweeping her cheeks, wondering why a
guy like him would be seriously interested in her when
he could take his pick of any of the stunning women
making a beeline straight for him.

'Chase! Oh, my, you get more gorgeous every time
I see you!'

The first blonde zeroed in on Chase, closely followed
by her friends and Lola sidled a foot away as the four
launched themselves at him, as he handled an armful
of beautiful blondes like any male would: with a wide
grin.

'And you must be Lola.'

The tallest blonde stuck out her hand. 'I'm Bron.
Wow, this week is going to be the best!'

'It should be fun,' she said, trying not to feel intimidated by all their tall perfection as each girl introduced
herself.

They seemed nice enough but she could tell by their
forced polite small talk and quick dismissive glances
they weren't interested in her, their attention quickly
snagged by one very handsome, very dashing guy dis-
cussing something with Cari as he furiously tapped
away at his smartphone before answering a call.

'What are you two hatching over there?'

Bron looped an arm through Cari's, who glared point-
edly at Chase before turning back to her friends.

'Nothing for you to worry about, Bron.'

Cari sent her a wink she had no chance of interpreting, before clapping her hands. 'Come on, girls. I'll show you to your rooms, then it's bubbly time.'

Lola inwardly grimaced. The last thing this effervescent lot needed was champagne.

As the girls followed Cari inside, Chase approached and she glanced at her watch, making a grand show of the fact she had work to do.

'I've got strict orders from Cari.'

Subduing an instant flare of panic that what she'd planned wouldn't be good enough for the bride-to-be's city chic friends, Lola winced. 'To start the party early?'

'To get you out of here.'

'What?'

'You heard me.'

He captured her hand and tugged her towards his car. 'Hen's orders.'

She stopped dead and tugged her hand to little avail. 'But…what…wait…I can't leave. The girls just arrived. I have to set up for the first session. There's a ton to do and—'

'Cari said the girls will take a few hours at least to catch up properly and ordered me to get you away for a while before the real chaos starts.'

Frowning, she mentally searched for more rational arguments and came up empty. 'In case you've forgotten, I'm being paid to handle that chaos.'

He squeezed her hand and her resistance melted a little more. 'Your job is to keep the hen happy and this is what Cari wants.'

Narrowing her eyes, she tried one last ploy. 'You know she's trying to matchmake? If you give in to her she'll have us up the aisle alongside her.'

There, that should send him running. It'd certainly worked last night, Cari's broad hints at matrimony effectively shutting him down.

Today, however, was another day.

'Let her have her fun. After our little discussion last night I'm under no illusions where I stand with you.'

Ouch. When put like that, he made her sound so callous, as if she'd rejected him and it still smarted. Then he smiled, a wicked grin that made her want to whack him.

'But hey, just so you know, I'm always up for a challenge.'

With a resigned huff, she tugged her hand free and marched towards the car before belatedly realising she didn't have her handbag with her.

'Just give me a minute to grab my bag.'

'Oh, no, you don't.'

He clamped an arm around her waist, effectively pinning her between his rock-hard body and the cool metal of his Jag.

'You go back in there and I doubt you'll come back out so hop in. You don't need a bag where we're going anyway.'

She started to struggle, saw the instant flare of desire in his eyes, felt the heat flood her body and she stilled.

If he saw her verbal refusal as a challenge, what would he think of her body squirming against his in her attempt to escape?

His mouth kicked up again and she had her answer. He'd definitely take it as an invitation and, giving him a shove, she managed to push him away and open the door at the same time.

'That's my girl,' he said, his mocking laughter making her yank the seat belt extra hard and jam it home.

Curiosity ate at her but she wouldn't give him the satisfaction of asking where he was taking her. Folding her arms, she stared resolutely out of the passenger window as he cruised down the driveway and out onto the highway.

'Seeing as you're not in a talkative mood, what would you like to listen to?'

'Whatever, you choose,' she said, embarrassed by her petulance. But being holed up in his car, his citrus aftershave blending with the heady scent of new leather, set her on edge.

She may have set the record straight last night but she now saw it for the futile exercise it was.

A guy like Chase wouldn't take no for an answer.

He would see it as a challenge, would pull out every trick in the book to woo her and for some strange reason his sister seemed to be in on the plan.

'You're not really mad at me, are you?'

His softly cajoling voice rippled over her and she stiffened, not wanting to give in too easily.

Not wanting to give in at all, damn it, but holding out against this man was like holding back a swarm of shoppers at the Boxing Day sales with a rope barrier—ineffectual at best.

Because she wasn't really mad at him, she was mad at herself for wanting to give in to him so badly.

Ignoring his question, she said, 'How long are you kidnapping me for?'

'A few hours.'

Glancing over his shoulder, he indicated and pulled onto a small lane just out of town.

'Don't worry, I'll have you back in plenty of time to keep the chooks busy.'

Unable to stay mad for long, she chuckled. 'Those girls are so far removed from being chooks it's not funny.'

'They like to think they are, getting all dolled up like that, but get them together in a group and they'll cackle till the sun comes up.'

And probably peck anyone who encroached on their territory. Strangely, that was how she'd felt for a moment or two when the girls had first descended on them—as if she was being sized up and found lacking for deigning to stand near Chase.

'Have you ever dated any of them?'

'Hell, no!'

His vehement response made her feel better than she should.

'Really? I would've thought successful, beautiful, bubbly women were your thing.'

He cast her a quizzical glance and she pretended to study the sound system.

'They're also demanding, narcissistic and to-tally headache-inducing. I like my women a lot less complicated.'

Great, so was he calling her simple?

The car slowed but for the life of her she couldn't make out anything of note in the surrounding bush.

'Not to mention they're Cari's friends and that's a definite no-go zone in the guys' handbook for appropriate dating.'

Ah…the real reason why he hadn't gone near any of the bombshell blonde foursome.

'As of yesterday, I'm Cari's friend too.'

Pulling over, he killed the engine and turned to face her, his expression surprisingly serious.

'That may be so, but *I* found you first.'

That shut her up and before she could come up with a suitable response, he said, 'Come on. Let's go kill a few hours.'

'But there's nothing here.'

'Yeah, there is.'

To her joy he opened her door for her, the second time he'd done it. The first had been when he'd taken her to that loft party but she'd been too dazed to really take notice of much but now his old-school display of manners thrilled her. If she had her way, chivalrous guys would make a comeback alongside daily gloves and hats.

'How do you feel about heights?'

'I'm not acrophobic if that's what you're asking.' She glanced around, noting they weren't on anything remotely resembling a mountain. 'Why? You planning on hang-gliding off this hillock?'

'No, I'm planning on taking you up in that.'

They rounded the trees and Lola's breath whooshed out in a rush as she caught sight of a huge hot air balloon.

'No way—'

'Come on, the pilot's waiting for us.'

Her look told him she didn't think the correct term for a hot-air balloon driver was pilot but she was too stunned to quibble.

'This is too…too…'

'Fun?' he helpfully supplied with a proud grin and she shook her head as they approached the monstrous basket.

'Too much,' she said, hanging back as he greeted the pilot like a long lost friend.

And it was too much. This reeked of a romantic date, something that took elaborate planning, a special event planned as a surprise by a caring boyfriend.

Confused and bamboozled and more than a tad excited she waited until he'd sorted out take-off plans with the pilot before asking, 'How did you do this?'

He slid his phone out of his pocket and brandished it. 'With this contraption you seem to hate so much. Bet you're glad you didn't confiscate it for ever now.'

'But when…?'

Of course, when she'd seen Cari and Chase deep in conversation while she'd been doing the round of introductions with the other girls, he'd been fiddling with his phone.

'You organised all this with that?' She swept her arm wide, encompassing the stunning view, before wrinkling her nose at the phone.

'You bet. You should try it some time. Move into the twenty-first century.'

'That's not the focus of my business.'

His gaze roved over her, taking in her navy broderie anglaise knee-length flared skirt cinched by a wide belt with an enamel bow, red and white striped sailor's top and flesh tone fishnets. She loved this French pirate look, wore it to feel jaunty and cheeky, two qualities she'd had a feeling she'd need today to deal with Cari's friends.

'Got to admit, there's something to be said for old stuff because you always look sensational.'

He probably paid compliments to women every day but having him appreciate the clothes she loved so much made her warm and gooey inside.

'You people ready for take-off?'

Chase nodded at the old guy fiddling with some ropes she hoped were sturdier than they looked.

He winked. 'See? Told you he was a pilot.'

'Keep up that smugness and I might just toss you over the side up there.'

She pointed to the cloudless sky, thankful for the lack of cumulus. While she didn't have acrophobia, going up in that basket was still a little hair-raising.

'You wouldn't do that.'

He captured her hand, ran his thumb over the back of it and she melted all the more inside.

She shouldn't be doing this, going on a romantic balloon ride, playing along with his flirting, letting him hold her hand. It reeked of romance and she was heading for a fall if she let herself believe any of this was real.

Yet as Chase helped her into the basket, popped a bottle of champagne on standby in a chiller and handed her a filled flute as the balloon slowly drifted upwards, she couldn't help but lose herself in the moment and wish it was.

'Pretty spectacular, huh?'

She gazed over the undulating hills far below, the

mountain ranges, the paddocks dotted with cows, determined to enjoy every moment of this surprise trip and not waste time second guessing Chase's motivation behind it.

When he didn't answer, she glanced to her left, only to discover he wasn't looking at the postcard view below them but was staring at her.

'Yeah. Spectacular.'

He raised his champagne flute in her direction, his slow, sexy smile totally disarming.

She couldn't look away, caught in the intensity of his stare, the beautiful blue rivalling the sky for clarity.

'What are you thinking?'

He tapped his champagne flute softly against hers and she gulped half of it to buy time.

What was she thinking? Stuff she shouldn't be.

Like how a girl could get used to this.

Like how the champagne and the altitude wasn't making her half as dizzy as having him stand close enough to touch.

Like how she wanted to renege on her previous stance of not mixing business with pleasure and go for it.

All the way.

'Never mind; you don't need to answer.'

He trailed a fingertip down her cheek in a sensuous caress that made her lungs seize. 'I can see the answer in your eyes.'

She quickly blinked but it was too late. Shareen had often teased her for being easy to read, every thought and feeling clearly visible in her eyes.

Time stood still as he leaned towards her, closer, closer, so close she could see the tiny green flecks in those stunning blue irises, so close she could smell his sexy crispness, so close she could feel the heat radiating off him and urging her to snuggle into his arms and never be cold again.

Her breath stalled as his head descended and, as her lips parted in expectation, he ducked towards her ear and murmured, 'Don't worry, I'm not going to push you. You need to want me as much as I want you.'

Rigid with tension, her hand trembled so much she lost some of her champagne over the side.

He wouldn't push her. She should be glad.

Instead, all she could think was how badly she yearned to be pushed into something so wrong for her yet something she wanted so much.

CHAPTER TEN

LOLA loved throwing retro parties. She loved the dress ups, the accessories, the make-up, the hair, loved seeing women play around with the things she treasured, loved seeing the smiles on their faces and their obvious enjoyment.

She'd had her doubts about the girls, expecting them to turn their collective noses up at the first activity she'd planned but to her relief they were throwing themselves wholeheartedly into the spirit of the afternoon.

'Hey Bry, your turn to try on that gingham/floral combo.'

Bryony preened in front of a mirror, twirling so the nineteen-twenties verdigris flapper dress flared at the hem, making the most of her long legs. 'Only if you try on that marabou feather dressing gown, Bron.'

Cari sidled her way between the two, looking chic in an Asian inspired peacock-blue bed jacket.

'Stop hogging the mirror, you two. House rules, the bride takes priority.'

They laughed, bumping and jostling for prime position as Babs and Binnie played around with sparkly shoe buckles and, glancing around the room, Lola's bubble of happiness expanded.

She'd been worried about this afternoon, worried about kicking off the hen's party with a good old-fashioned dress up and no amount of drifting through the sky, high on hot air and Chase's charm, had dispelled it.

But seeing the smiles on these girls' faces, their genuine joy, hearing their laughter, boded well for the rest of the week.

'Hey Lola, what's this thing for?'

Cari held up a snood and, called into the fray, Lola spent the next hour doling out handy hints on wearing a snood versus a beret, ways to cinch your waist and still be able to breathe and being able to walk not mince in a Chinese silk dress.

The girls lapped it up and by the end of the session, when the last hat pin and brooch had been packed away, she collapsed onto the sofa alongside them, sipping her third champagne for the day and not caring a bit.

She listened to the girls' banter, content to sit and let their conversation flow over her, desultory and humorous and easy-going.

It lulled her and after the day she'd had she could've quite happily curled up here for the rest of the evening and not moved.

'So Lola, what's your story?'

Just like that, her serenity vanished. She didn't like talking about herself, didn't like being the centre of attention.

She'd spent too much time as a kid and a teenager trying to avoid being just that yet scrutinised anyway, from the way she dressed to what she ate to who she brought or didn't bring home.

She'd hated every under-the-microscope second and despite the image she'd carefully cultivated over the years having these gorgeous, confident, well put together women turn their attention on her made her want to run screaming.

Regretting that last champagne and what it might make her blab, she shrugged.

'Not much to tell. Born and bred in Brisbane, got tired of the heat, headed south to Melbourne after I finished school and got a business diploma, took a chance on the vintage stuff I loved, opened my own place and I've been spending all my time building Go Retro since.'

Babs sniggered. 'That's all well and good, but what about boys? Is there anyone special in your life? Any juicy stories?'

Lola tried to dispel the image of Chase that popped into her head with little success.

'Go Retro keeps me pretty busy.'

Bryony finished off the rest of her champagne in a long gulp and jabbed a finger at her. 'We're all busy, darl, but that doesn't stop us from having the odd story in our past. Come on, 'fess up, one boy story or we won't leave you alone.'

Lola glanced in Cari's direction for help but she merely shrugged and raised her champagne flute in a silent toast.

Knowing she'd have to give the girls something or they'd never let up, she screwed up her nose, pretending to think. 'Well, there was this one guy...'

Babs clapped her hands. 'We knew it! Tell all.'

Not wanting to tread too far down memory lane for

fear of blurting the whole sorry truth about Bodey, she settled for an abbreviated version.

'I'd been in Melbourne a few months, met this cool guy at a local café. He asked me out, we dated for a month, then things cooled off.'

She left out how smooth Bodey was, how he'd showered her with compliments and taken her to trendy jazz bars and fancy restaurants, plying her with attention that she'd lapped up. She'd taken it slow, waiting a month to sleep with him, so sure he had visions of a long-term relationship.

After that one night together, he'd never returned her calls. And she'd learned a valuable life lesson: that if it looked too good and sounded too good it probably was too good to be true.

Bryony shrugged. 'His loss.'

Bron chirped up. 'Yeah, not that you'd be single for long. Guys would take one look at you in those clothes and instantly think Marilyn Monroe. You'd have them lining up.'

Binnie shot her an envious glance. 'Wish I had your killer curves.'

Blushing, Lola tried not to squirm. These girls barely knew her but they were lavish in their compliments. Why couldn't her own family have seen what these girls had in less than a day?

'Er…thanks…'

'Leave Lola alone; can't you see you're embarrassing her?'

She sent Cari a grateful smile.

'Now, if you want gossip, I'll tell you who Hugh ran

into at the races last week. Remember Jason Virstock the third? Well…'

Cari winked as she successfully distracted the girls, leaving Lola to slip out of the room and into the kitchen to check their special dinner.

But as she ensured the fondue was ready to go and the pigs-in-blankets were in the oven, she couldn't help but lament her lack of juicy gossip.

She'd played it safe her entire life. Staying in the shadows, out of her sister's limelight, too scared some of it may reflect onto her. She didn't want people fawning over her or schmoozing up to her because of how she looked.

As for guys, she wanted a guy for the long haul, who loved the old-fashioned stuff as much as she did. A guy who made her feel…just like how Chase made her feel.

With a wistful sigh, she stabbed at a cocktail onion and cheese cube with a toothpick and stuck it into an overturned cabbage, an hors d'oeuvre taken straight out of a nineteen-fifties cookbook.

Yeah, she loved how Chase made her feel.

Pity he couldn't be the guy for her.

Chase hated feeling superfluous so after the first two days when the girls had been caught up in a whirlwind of facials and fondue and frocks he'd headed back to Melbourne, determined to bury himself in business and forget about luscious Lola.

That balloon ride had been too close for comfort.

What had begun as a mission to give Lola a bit of breathing space before the week-long party started in earnest had resulted in a romantic interlude he couldn't forget.

And he'd tried, boy, had he tried. He didn't want to remember the way the wind had blown her soft blonde curls around her face, the way her eyes had sparkled during the entire journey, the way she'd unconsciously leaned against him during the descent, as if needing his reassurance.

At the time he'd lapped it up, enjoying their time together and surprised by how seriously relaxing he'd found a balloon ride drifting through the sky to be.

Yet looking back he knew the romantic touches like the champagne had been a mistake; for he didn't have room in his life for romance. Some light-hearted fun, not a problem, but anything deeper? No, thanks, and he had a niggling feeling Lola was a deep and meaningful kinda girl.

His aim to forget had worked at the office as he'd caught up on urgent business but once darkness descended and he headed to his penthouse he'd found himself hating the silence, hating the solitude and most of all hating the fact he was missing a woman he barely knew.

He'd deliberately gone out that night to a modelling agency party where he'd provided the high-end lighting and music technicians. Determined to blow off Lola's memory, he'd surrounded himself with beautiful women, the type of women he usually found riveting enough to date.

It didn't work.

As a distraction technique the evening had been an unmitigated disaster. Rather than flirting, he'd found himself clutching the same drink in his hand for the first hour while he feigned interest in stick-thin, ambitious women who'd do anything to get to the top.

He understood ambition.

He understood this glamorous world.

What he didn't understand was the gnawing drive to walk out of the party and head straight for Mount Macedon.

He'd thrown himself into work harder the next day, not stopping until ten-thirty when the nightly cleaner knocked on his door and only then had he dragged himself home.

On the third day, after another sleepless night, he gave up and headed back. It was his house after all. Only fair he check on it and make sure the girls weren't running amok, right?

He cringed at his lousy excuses as he let himself into the house, following the sounds of laughter coming from the atrium out the back.

When he'd had the house designed by Melbourne's top architect he'd gone with the guy's plans for a sprawling family home even though he had no intention of filling it in that way. The way he saw it, the house would be a testament to what he would never make the mistake of falling for: an empty dream that sucked you in but never delivered on its promise.

Yet whenever he entered the atrium he couldn't help but think it begged to be filled with a couple of rowdy kids and a rambunctious dog cavorting around in the sun-filled, glass-enclosed family room.

The girls were sprawled on the blue and white striped divans, looking happy and relaxed as they watched Lola demonstrate the art of making a giant roll with a section of her hair and pinning it on the top.

'Voila, the pin curl,' she said, her bubbly voice sending a shot of longing through him so strong he clutched onto the door jamb for support. 'Come on, time for you to try it.'

As the girls reached for bobby pins, Bron sat still, a frown crinkling her forehead as she studied Lola.

'You remind me of someone with your hair like that.'

Lola's hand stilled, the hairbrush in her right hand hovering over Cari's head, her expression carefully blank but not before he'd seen a flicker of fear.

He didn't understand it. What did she have to be frightened about?

Babs elbowed Bron. 'A pin-up girl from the fifties, you dolt.'

Bron shook her head, then tilted it to one side to study Lola more carefully. 'No, someone else. It's been bugging me all week but just then, when you lifted your hair back off your face it really hit me, but I can't think who…'

Lola paled and he could've sworn her hand shook as she lowered the hairbrush, her shoulders rigid as she turned slightly on the pretext of grabbing more hairpins, the move perfectly executed as a curtain of hair fell forward to partially conceal her face.

He'd never seen her like this. She'd always been confident and brash, discounting the times he'd kissed her, but they'd both been pretty bamboozled then.

No, this was different and he took a step into the room to lend her a hand.

'Come on, Lola, work with me,' Bron said, and as Lola shot her a quick glance Bron jumped up from her seat and snapped her fingers.

'That's it! You look like that supermodel Shareen. Oh my goodness, when you just looked at me with your hair falling forward like that, you were the spitting image.'

The hairbrush in Lola's hand clattered to the floor as Bron gushed and in that moment Chase knew something was seriously wrong.

'You're related, aren't you?'

Lola gnawed on her bottom lip before nodding. 'She's my sister.'

Bron grabbed her arm and spun her around. 'Your sister? Wow! You never said. Now that I've nailed it, you're so alike. I knew something about you looked familiar but I never thought…I mean, she's a supermodel and you're…'

'Nothing like her. Yeah, so I've been told.'

Chase's heart plummeted as he saw Lola's face crumple for a second before she quickly masked her distress with a performance worthy of an Oscar, her expression one of studied concentration as she picked up the hairbrush and ran it through Cari's hair with firm, practised strokes as if the last thirty seconds hadn't happened.

Bron folded her arms. 'Well, those people were wrong. You are alike; you've got the same bone structure and facial expressions, and what I was going to say was she's a supermodel but you're one of us.'

Cari nodded. 'Yeah, and I'd much rather run a vintage shop and do the fun stuff you do than strut around wearing impossibly high heels and completely unrealistic fashion.'

'Me too,' Babs and Binnie piped up in unison.

Chase didn't know why revealing Shareen was her sister had spooked Lola so much but, looking at her now, he admired the way she'd straightened her shoulders and tossed her hair back, as if it mattered little.

'Shareen and I are just very different people. I don't talk about her much because it's not relevant to what I do.'

Bron shot her a sceptical look but wisely kept silent after her earlier interrogation.

'Now, how about you practice pinning those curls while I go make us some fresh coffee?'

The girls groaned good-naturedly and he almost laughed out loud, until he saw her expression crumble again as she turned away from them.

She'd taken three steps towards the kitchen when she caught sight of him and to his horror her bottom lip quivered.

Holding his finger up to his lips, he pointed to the kitchen and she hesitated a moment before reluctantly nodding.

Time enough to greet the girls. For now, he needed to discover what the famous Shareen had done to rattle her beautiful sister so much.

Mortification didn't come close to describing Lola's feelings as she slipped into the kitchen to find Chase waiting for her.

With a little luck Chase hadn't heard her secret revealed.

'You just got back?'

'About ten minutes ago.'

Great, there went that theory.

She wanted to bolt and hide but just the sight of this man made her want to run into his arms instead, which took the decision to tell him the truth out of her hands.

'You heard?'

He nodded, worry clouding those incredible blue eyes she'd seen filled with mischief and heat and desire.

'Guess you want to know why I kept Shareen a secret too?'

He shrugged and joined her at the granite island bench taking centre stage in the kitchen.

'It's your business. Don't let those women railroad you into anything.'

She wrinkled her nose as she arranged coffee cups on a tray. 'It was kind of embarrassing, though. Like I'd been trying to hide something.'

He placed the sugar bowl and teaspoons alongside the mugs. 'Like you said, it's irrelevant.'

She snorted. 'Wish the great Shareen could hear you say that.' Waiting for the espresso machine to do its thing, she propped herself on a stool tucked under the bench. 'My sister may be many things; irrelevant isn't one of them.'

Watching his face, trying to gauge his reaction, she said, 'Did you know she's the third highest paid super-model in the world this year?'

And she couldn't even make enough to guarantee she could meet her payments on next year's mortgage on Go Retro. Not that she begrudged Shareen her success—she'd worked hard for all she'd achieved. Starving her-self for years, working out for hours daily, forgoing any kind of treats the rest of Australia's female population took for granted. But she worked hard too and for once she wished it paid off.

To his credit, Chase's expression didn't change. He didn't seem overly impressed or bedazzled as most guys were.

'Money isn't everything.'

'Spoken like a guy who has plenty of it.'

His eyes widened a fraction. 'You're in financial strife?'

Damn, what was it about this guy that invited her confidences?

'Not really. Just the usual ever-increasing mortgage and creative accounting and juggling books running a small business requires.'

She waited for a monetary offer, something a take charge guy like him would do, an offer that would make her feel less competent than she already did. But to his credit he merely nodded, his expression thoughtful.

'So why'd you panic in there?'

She grimaced. 'You saw that, huh?'

'Yeah, though you masked it well from the others.'

He studied her closely and she struggled not to squirm under his scrutiny. 'Though from where I was standing, looked like you were pretty shaken up admitting Shareen's your sister.'

She sighed and cast a hopeful glance at the espresso machine but sadly it was still doing its thing and couldn't save her.

With a reluctant sigh, she slumped against the island bench. 'Till I came to Melbourne I spent most of my life being compared to my sister. When my folks weren't doing it, their friends were. Everywhere we went, people would compare the two of us.'

And find her lacking.

She didn't have to say it. He saw the truth written all over her face despite her best efforts to hide her bitterness.

'You're beautiful—'

'I was a toad next to my sister. She's tall, I'm average. She's a rake, I'm a blob—'

'Now, wait just a minute.' He slid his hands around her waist before she could move and her traitorous body stayed put, loving the contact. 'Don't do that, undersell yourself.'

His hands slid around to the small of her back, bringing her body temptingly close to his.

'Your curves are gorgeous. You're feminine and stunning and they drive me wild.'

She opened her mouth to protest and he swooped, his lips silencing her with a devastating kiss that made a mockery of every self-loathing thought she'd ever had.

When Chase kissed her, she felt beautiful.

She felt like a woman who'd never cried herself to sleep because she couldn't fit into her sister's designer hand-me-downs.

She felt like a woman who'd never had to forgo her beloved chocolate mousse at a party because her mother was frowning at her over the dessert table.

She felt like a woman who could genuinely attract a man like Chase.

It was keeping him that would be the problem.

Easing away, she placed her palms against his chest.

'You sure know how to distract a girl.'

His mouth quirked into a smile that made her breathless all over again.

'I wasn't aiming for distraction.'

'Could've fooled me.'

Capturing her face between his hands to ensure she didn't break eye contact, he brushed a soft kiss against her lips. 'I was proving a point. You're a desirable woman, Lola. Every gorgeous inch of you.'

'Spoken like a man who's after something he can't have.'

She mentally kicked herself the moment the words were out as he swore and released her.

'You think I'm trying to sweet-talk you into bed?'

Hating that she'd shattered the cosiness of a moment ago, she cocked an eyebrow. 'Aren't you?'

'No…yes…hell…' He jammed a hand through his hair, raking it into a rarely seen muss.

'I've never made any secret of wanting you but that wasn't what this was about.'

Surprised by the wild, out of control glint in his eyes, she slid to her feet, pushing the stool back under the island bench.

'Then what's this about?'

He paced several steps, muttering under his breath before swivelling to face her, his wild-eyed look undiminished.

'I came back because I missed you, dammit. I couldn't think straight, I couldn't concentrate at work, I couldn't sleep for—'

He bit back the rest of what he was going to say but

she needed to hear it, her heart swelling with joy at his honesty.

'For?'

Reluctantly dragging his gaze to meet hers, he blurted, 'For wanting to be near you.'

Not *wanting you*, as she'd originally thought as his only motivation for being so nice to her.

Wanting to be near you.

Even now she doubted his sincerity, taking his words as a tried and true line he'd probably used on countless women but one look at his face, at the vulnerability underlying every hard plane, showed every word had been genuine.

Clenching his hands by his sides, he muttered, 'Say something.'

Taking a step forward, she cupped his cheek, reining in her rampant yearning to wrap her arms around him and never let go. 'Thank you.'

He remained rigid for a long moment before relaxing into her hand and they stood there for a perfect, exquisite moment before the espresso machine signalled it was time to get back to the real world.

Not that she cared.

After what he'd just said, she'd be floating for the rest of the day.

Lola swanned into the glamour session the next morning, grinning as five collective jaws dropped.

'Oh, my, what are you wearing?' Cari gasped. 'I have to have it!'

For once, the four Bs were speechless as she pirouetted and twirled to show off the dress.

'This, my friends, is a vintage floral print silky satin bubble gown with a hand-beaded and lightly boned bodice.'

Bryony whistled. 'You look like you've been poured into it.'

'Remember that cinching session we did the other day?' Lola smiled and tapped her waist. 'You too can fool the masses with an old-fashioned corset.'

As the girls fussed around her, feeling the luxurious material, Cari elbowed her. 'Has Chase seen you in this yet? Because when he does, watch out.'

Lola pretended not to hear, ignoring Cari's chuckles as she shooed them to take a seat.

She'd had another sleepless night courtesy of Chase and his declaration.

I couldn't sleep for wanting to be near you.

Well, the feeling was entirely mutual and, no matter how much she reminded herself of their differences, she couldn't stop thinking about him, couldn't stop wanting him to look at her in that special way.

Wearing her favourite dress today hadn't been about impressing Chase; it merely symbolised how great she felt—on top of the world, a woman preening beneath the admiration of an amazing guy.

Clapping her hands, she said, 'Okay, let's get started. Today is all about glamour. What it means, what you can do to add a little in your daily life with simple touches.'

Babs pointed a black patent designer sandal her way. 'That's easy. Colour coordinate with Jimmy or Christian every day.'

The girls laughed.

'While those shoes are gorgeously glam, for those who can't afford them, here are a few tricks of the trade.'

Lola whipped off a sheet covering a table loaded with knick-knacks she used for her glamour presentation, enjoying the 'ooooh's in unison.

'So far, we've dealt with your basic stuff to make you feel glamorous: red lipstick, garters, seamed stockings, sky-high heels and how to wiggly walk in them, pin curls, victory rolls, finger waves and make-up.'

Gesturing at the table, she said, 'But glamour isn't all about perfect hair and make-up. With a few choice accessories, you can feel truly special.'

Her fingers drifted over the feathers, the lace, the silk flowers, loving the sensory experience as much as the familiarity of much loved items.

'It's easy to add a few glamorous touches when you're dressed up and ready for work or a night out. But what about those days you're lounging around at home, maybe feeling a tad under the weather?'

Preaching to a captive audience, she held up a bold marigold, aqua and claret silk scarf.

'Having a bad hair day? Just run a brush through it and tie it up with a beautiful scarf like this. Or you can try headband style or go Audrey Hepburn-esque and cover your whole head.'

She held up a small lace-trimmed amethyst satin pillow. 'Always surround yourself with rich fabrics. Satin covers, lace frills, soft cottons, are perfect for snuggling up with as you read, watch TV, lounge around, whatever.'

Holding up a sheer pearl silk nightgown, she waited

for the wolf whistles to stop before continuing. 'And speaking of lounging around, sensual fabrics shouldn't be reserved for impressing guys. Pretty nighties, feather-trimmed bed jackets, socks with bows, anything super girly can make you feel pampered and glam, even if the only person enjoying it is you.'

Passing around the nightgown and pillow, she picked up a hand-painted teacup. 'In this era of lattes and fancy mocha-chinos, we've lost the art of savouring quality tea. Using a beautiful porcelain teacup like this one not only brings out the true flavour of the tea but makes you feel just a little bit royal.'

She laughed as Babs mimicked holding up a teacup, pinkie extended.

'I guess what I'm trying to emphasise here is we can take a leaf out of the old days. Whether it be a bunch of fresh-cut flowers from the garden or a hand-me-down nana blanket or a store-bought scented candle, all these items can bring a little bit of glamour and pampering into our lives.'

Pausing, she kinked out her hip in a theatrical move that elicited more whistling and hoots. 'After all, we deserve it.'

The girls clapped and crowded around her, jostling for position as they played with her props.

Rapt that they'd enjoyed another session, she stood back, answering questions, content to watch the women appreciate vintage while clad in head to toe modern.

There was much jesting and a few ribald sugges-tions as Bryony held up the sheer nightgown against Cari and, in that instant, Lola was transported out of Chase's cavernous lounge room and into his bedroom, imagining what he would do if he saw her in something like that…

A hot blush scorched her cheeks and she quickly turned away, but not before Binnie caught sight of her.

'Looks like Cari's not the only one conjuring up visions of a honeymoon night.'

Aghast she was that easy to read, Lola managed a tight smile, mumbled something about getting refreshments, and headed for the safety of the kitchen and a nice cold drink filled with ice. Plenty of ice.

Chase had it bad.

He didn't chase women; women came after him. It wasn't vanity, it was fact and something he'd taken for granted.

Until now.

For the woman he wanted so badly he ached wouldn't chase him unless he threatened to dress the local wallabies in her vintage dress collection.

Sure, they'd grown closer over the last few days, snatching coffees between manicure sessions and managing a late night supper after a tarot evening, but Lola still remained slightly aloof, as if she was holding out on him.

Or was afraid.

He'd seen her fear, whenever they'd got too close. After every kiss, she'd looked as if she wanted to bolt, as if she didn't believe any of it was real.

From what she'd told him about her sister, he understood. She had body image issues, growing up in the shadow of a supermodel. Probably had her self-esteem battered by the constant comparisons she'd talked about.

But he'd done everything in his power to convince her she was a desirable, beautiful woman in her own right. Was that the problem? He'd only been using words. Was it time to take action?

From their chats he figured Go Retro was what mattered most to her. Plus she'd mentioned financial woes—something about a mortgage—what if he could show her how much she meant to him by helping her with her prized possession?

He knew she didn't accept help easily. She'd refused to let the girls lift a finger all week, had categorically told him to back off when he'd offered to help her set up for a few sessions and she'd insisted on running into town and stocking up on essentials herself despite a phone-in home delivery service he used when up here.

He admired her independence even if it chafed not to be able to help out when she needed it. Yet if she needed help for Go Retro, her pride and joy, to stay viable, surely she'd bend her rules and accept some well-meaning assistance?

An idea glimmered into his consciousness and with a jubilant fist pump he reserved for scoring major coups at Dazzle, he reached for the phone.

It took him less than five minutes to set his plan in motion and when he hung up his first instinct was to go and find Lola and tell her the good news.

However, one glance at the hen's party itinerary sitting on his desk scuttled that idea. She'd be in the middle of preparing for the final dinner party and no way would he get between those girls and their food.

Though he should be glad Cari had enjoyed this so much. He'd never seen his sister so relaxed, let alone not ringing the office ten times a day as he was also prone to do.

Thankfully, she'd eased off on the matchmaking stakes but only after he'd told her he had it under control, which she took to mean he was actively pursuing Lola and needed no assistance.

Little did she know that Lola had him so bewildered he didn't know whether to bolt back to Melbourne or hide away in his study here.

And therein lay the kicker.

For all his chivalrous notion of helping her out to show her he was more than a shallow playboy, he had no idea what he'd do if she actually believed he liked her.

He did, there was no doubt, but realistically once they returned to the city tomorrow he should call it quits. Pursuing her would lead nowhere. With her old-fashioned outlook, she wanted more than he was willing to give and despite their heated kisses, no way would she be satisfied with a fling.

Considering how close they'd grown over the last week, maybe it was for the best they let this *thing* between them fizzle out.

He'd accompany her to the Hotel Antiqua opening, get her business back on track and bow out gracefully. No harm, no foul.

Then why did he have a hard time believing it?

Lola cradled a mug of cocoa between her hands and tucked her feet under her. The divan on the back veranda had become her favourite hideaway over the last week whenever she needed some downtime, the soft, plump cushions so tempting she could fall asleep.

The final dinner party had gone off without a hitch: the good old-fashioned food—prawn cocktails, Beef Wellington, trifle, soda fountains and Death by Chocolate mousse—had been a hit. Soon, she'd fire up the big band music and the girls would learn a few ballroom dance steps and that'd be the end of her duties.

The week had been a rousing success and she should be ecstatic. Instead, she couldn't help but feel a twinge of regret it had come to an end. Imogen had run Go Retro without a hiccup and in a way it had been nice to take a break from the constant pressure of making her business flourish.

She lived and breathed the shop, lovingly attending to the merchandise during the day while juggling the books with gritted teeth at night. She'd cut corners wherever possible while not compromising the quality of stock but the retail industry had hit tough times and despite the reprieve from running this party, she constantly worried if her beloved shop would be ripped away one day.

Immy had offered to be joint partner but her pride wouldn't allow it. She didn't want her friend investing, didn't want to accept the fact she couldn't do this on her own. For if she accepted Immy's offer, where would it stop? Would she end up approaching her family for financial assistance in the future? No way in hell. She'd rather shut up shop than ask for help from the people who'd only be too happy to say, *We told you so*.

Thankfully, Cari had loved every minute of the hen's party and apparently she had four future customers in the other girls when their turn came to traipse up the aisle. Word of mouth was the best kind of advertising and if the girls had their way she'd be getting referrals for a while yet. Throw in the exorbitant fee she was being paid and she should be over the moon.

Taking a sip of cocoa and savouring the smooth chocolate on her tongue, she knew her reticence had everything to do with never seeing a tall blue-eyed charmer again.

Quite simply, she'd miss Chase.

Miss his teasing, his compliments, his smiles.

Miss his interesting conversation, his attentiveness, his kisses.

Whenever she'd been with him over the last week he'd made her feel as if she was special, as if she was the only woman in the world and for that alone she was tempted to throw caution to the wind and see if he wanted to catch up again in Melbourne.

But they were two different people from different worlds and she knew the moment they got back to the city they'd go their separate ways.

Chase belonged in his glass tower on swank Collins Street; she belonged in her old retro shop on Errol Street. A hip, contemporary guy didn't belong with an old-fashioned girl. And all the smooth compliments and suave smiles in the world couldn't change that.

'Thought I might find you out here.'

Lola smiled at Cari and shuffled over to make room for her. 'Ready to boogie?'

'Don't you mean waltz?'

'With the music I've got lined up, you girls will be dancing your feet off all night.'

Cari cast her a mischievous wink. 'Sure Chase can't join in? You two could demonstrate some dirty dancing.'

Lola blushed and hid behind her cocoa mug.

'He likes you, you know.'

Lola muttered a non-committal answer and continued to sip her cocoa.

'I've never seen him like this.'

Cari bunched up her knees and wrapped her arms around them, completely at home squished up on the sofa next to her and it struck Lola how she'd never done this with Shareen. Just hung out, the two of them at home, exchanging confidences, casually chatting.

She would've liked to, for she'd adored her older sister. Until she'd turned into a stuck-up cow who wouldn't smile unless she got paid for it.

Curious to hear Cari's perspective on her brother's romantic endeavours yet kicking herself for caring, she continued to sip her cocoa, hoping her silence would be all the encouragement Cari needed. Thankfully, it was.

'Sure, he's done his fair share of dating. Nothing serious.' Cari paused, shot her a sly grin. 'And I've never seen him look at anyone the way he looks at you.'

'That's because I'm a challenge,' she said, wishing she'd remained silent when Cari shook her head, her grin replaced by a frown.

'Do you always do that, sell yourself short? Because you shouldn't. You're a successful, attractive businesswoman.' Cari glared for good measure. 'And nobody gives a rat's if your sister is a supermodel. You're the one we know and love.'

Lola choked on her cocoa, the sting of tears prickling her eyes.

How could this go-getter, savvy corporate lawyer say something so right and mean it, when her own family didn't recognise her worth?

'Chase said something similar.'

Cari snapped her fingers. 'There you go. Two smart Etheridges can't be wrong.'

'You won't be an Etheridge for much longer.'

Cari glowed whenever any mention of Hugh or the wedding came up.

'Actually, that's why I came out here.'

'Oh?'

'Wanted to catch you in a quiet moment before we wind up tonight and you rush off tomorrow.'

Lola gnawed on her bottom lip. Was she that easy to read? For that was exactly what she'd planned on doing, packing the last few boxes in the van at the crack of dawn and making a hasty getaway before she could be drawn into awkward goodbyes with a sexy CEO who could probably get her to stay with a lazy smile.

'I'd like you to come to the wedding.'

Lola's mouth dropped open before she realised how ridiculous she looked and snapped it shut, as Cari held up her hand to stave off any potential refusal.

'In my line of work, I don't get a lot of downtime so I don't socialise much. When I do, it's with those crazy four in there, girls I've worked with for years.'

For the first time since they'd met, Cari appeared uncomfortable as she squirmed in the seat before releasing her legs and sitting upright.

'What I'm trying to say is, I don't make friends easily,

Lola. I don't have the time or the inclination. But this past week has been great and I feel like I've known you as long as the four Bs. So what do you say? Will you come?'

Speechless, Lola swallowed the lump of emotion in her throat. 'But it's a small wedding, close friends and family—'

'I don't even know if my own parents will show up so apart from Chase the family thing is moot. I want you there.'

Distracted from her dilemma from a moment, she tried to make sense of what Cari had just said.

'Your folks aren't coming?'

Cari shrugged, a wealth of hurt in her face. 'They RSVP'd to the invite but with them you never know. Apparently they've got some graduation thing on the same day. Wouldn't put it past them to decide to attend that at the last minute instead.'

'But isn't your mum…' She bit back the rest of what she was going to say, understanding the pain Cari was going through, empathising completely.

If she got married, would her mum be helping her choose a dress and flowers and catering? Not likely.

Was that why Chase was organising the hen's party too? He'd said it was because his sister had everything and he wanted to do something special, something out of the ordinary, but was it because their mother didn't care enough to be involved in her only daughter's wedding?

'We've never been close so she isn't involved in the wedding.' Cari picked at a fraying thread on the cushion she hugged to her chest.

'Chase practically raised me. We had nannies early on but once he was deemed old enough he picked me up from school, cooked dinner, helped me with my homework. He was amazing.'

Trying not to pry but shocked that the two successful Etheridges had had such a stark upbringing, she said, 'Where were your folks?'

'At the university. They're professors there. They basically lived there, using our house as a place to sleep whatever hour they came in.'

Cari clutched the cushion tighter. 'When Chase and I were young it wasn't too bad. We'd do some family stuff at the uni after school. Picnics and walks mostly. But once Chase hit his early teens and could look after me and fend for himself, they withdrew, spending more time at work.'

Lola didn't blame Cari for her audible bitterness. She knew exactly what it was like to be ignored by your parents.

'Now you can understand why having family at the wedding isn't all important but I do want friends, people who mean something to me, to be there.'

When Lola opened her mouth to protest Cari made a zipping motion over her lips.

'And that includes you.'

'Are you sure? I'm not—'

Cari's eyes narrowed. 'No underselling, remember?'

With a rueful chuckle, Lola finally nodded. 'I'd love to come. Thanks for the invite.'

Cari let out a whoop and hugged her and this time she fought a losing battle with the tears.

It wasn't until they'd both swiped their eyes and she followed Cari back into the house to get the dancing underway did she realise that her intentions of making a clean break from Chase once she left here had just gone up in a cloud of confetti.

CHAPTER ELEVEN

LOLA loved dancing. She loved the fluidity, the sensuality, the ability to lose herself in the music.

She loved how people of any shape or size could seemingly float across the dance floor looking elegant and light-footed.

And she especially loved the rhythm pulsing through her body, making her feet itch to get out there and join whoever happened to be dancing.

Except tonight.

Tonight, she'd intended on being the teacher, putting to good use the lessons she'd had when she'd first moved to Melbourne and opened Go Retro.

She'd wanted to offer full service parties and as part of her packages she included old-style dancing. Anything from the waltz to the foxtrot, the Pride of Erin to the Charleston, she could do it all and dancing was the one time she never felt self-conscious about her size.

Until Chase Etheridge walked in the room and propped himself against the wall at the start of the first lesson.

'Hang on a sec, girls, back in a tic.'

One of the Bs sniggered as she marched across to Chase, whose grin widened as she approached.

'Don't mind me, I'm here to pick up a few pointers.'

Stifling the urge to smile right back, she tried a frown for good measure.

'I don't perform to an audience.'

'Oh, I wasn't here to just watch.'

Before she realised his intention, he'd snagged her hand and tugged her closer, before spinning her out and back again, leaving her breathless.

'When I said I want pointers, I want first-hand instruction from the teacher.'

Trying to ignore the clapping and cheering from the girls, she pushed against his chest.

'I don't need a partner to teach, thanks.'

He pretended to consider this but she could see the mischief shifting in his eyes. He was up to something.

'Shame, because the rest of the girls will be partnered up and I didn't want you to feel left out.'

'Partnered?'

She jumped as he whistled, a short, shrill call followed by what sounded like a herd of stampeding cattle coming down the hallway.

When five guys burst into the room and Cari shrieked, she narrowed her eyes and glared.

'This is a hen's party. Where'd the famous five come from?'

'See for yourself.'

Lola turned in time to see Cari fly into the arms of the tallest guy, a redhead, and kiss him silly, while the four girls didn't waste time introducing themselves to the other guys.

When Cari and Hugh finally disengaged, Cari looked so radiant she didn't have the heart to chastise Chase further.

'Where'd the posse come from?'

Chase raised his hand in a casual wave that only guys could pull off when trying to act cool.

'Hugh's mates. Guys he's invited to the wedding, I presume. I called him up, said Cari was pining and would love to have him and some mates join the girls on the last night for a bit of serious booty shaking.'

She jabbed him in the chest. 'That's false advertising. We're doing old-style stuff, not Latin American.'

'We can improvise.'

Sliding an arm around her waist and tugging her close, he murmured in her ear, 'I quite fancy seeing you shake your—'

'This must be Lola.'

Trying to squirm out of Chase's grip and failing, she managed a tight smile for Hugh, who was nothing like what she'd imagined. Somehow, she'd envisaged Cari with tall, dark and handsome, and the closest she'd got was with the tall.

Hugh had bright blue eyes and red hair and a smattering of freckles that made him look ten years old, yet she knew from Cari's chats he was a thirty-two-year-old corporate lawyer constantly underestimated by his peers and courtroom foes.

'Nice to meet you.'

'Likewise.'

She smiled and stuck out her hand, engulfed in his but thankfully not squeezed too hard before he released it. 'So you guys up for some dancing tonight?'

Hugh pulled a face and lowered his voice as he glanced over his shoulder and saw Cari making a bee-line for them. 'I loathe anything involving my two left feet but my bride-to-be is insisting on dance lessons so thought it wouldn't hurt to get in a bit of practice tonight.'

'Brave man.'

Chase clapped him on the back as Cari joined their group and hooked her arm through Hugh's, gazing up at him in obvious adoration.

When Hugh glanced down and their eyes locked, communicating some silent sweet message that had them both blushing, a lump formed in Lola's throat.

What would it be like to be in sync with a guy? To be totally on the same wavelength that you didn't have to speak to convey thoughts?

She'd love to find someone like that, someone who openly adored her yet would be happy with the real her, the woman behind the pin curls and red lipstick.

She'd never met any guy she'd been willing to reveal herself to, never come close.

And Chase chose that moment to slip his hand into hers and gently squeeze, as if sensing her thoughts and the lump in her throat grew to boulder proportions.

'Looks like the gang over there is still busy with introductions. Why don't we wait fifteen minutes then get started?'

Shooting Chase a grateful glance, Lola watched Cari and Hugh do their eye contact thing again, as if words weren't necessary.

'Fine with me,' Cari said, snuggling closer to Hugh. 'Gives us a few minutes to catch up.'

'That's what they're calling it these days,' Chase muttered, masking his cheek with a discreet cough when Cari glared.

'Come on, hun, I'll show you the flowers I've chosen.'

As Cari tugged Hugh towards the door in a hurry, Chase murmured, 'Bet those pics are in her bedroom.'

Hugh grinned and gave him a thumbs up while Cari tilted her chin higher and pretended not to hear.

Waving a hand at the four Bs doing their best to match up with Hugh's mates, Chase said, 'Want to get some air?'

'Yeah, why not?'

Belatedly realising they were still holding hands, Lola let Chase lead her to the atrium, her favourite place inside the house during the day when sunlight flooded through the floor to ceiling glass.

Now, as they stepped inside and she reached for the light switch, Chase stilled her hand.

'It's better this way.'

Lola had no idea what he was referring to but her heart pounded in anticipation as he led her deeper into the cavernous room and tugged her down on a chaise longue beside him.

'Look up.'

She craned her neck, only momentarily resisting when he eased her back so her head rested on his shoulder, his arms sliding around her middle to cradle her close.

'Wow,' she breathed out on a sigh, blinking and refocusing at the twinkling stars scattered across the midnight-blue sky.

'Yeah, wow,' he echoed and as she tilted her head

slightly, she realised he was looking at her, not the stunning solar show overhead.

A raging battle took place between her head and her heart.

Head: 'What the heck do you think you're doing? Last night, remember? Clean break? Hello?'

Heart: 'When he holds you like this, couldn't you just stay this way for ever?'

Head: 'Dummy, there's no such thing as forever with a guy like him.'

Heart: 'Yeah, but being in his arms feels so good. This is the last time, must savour it.'

Head: 'Sheesh, don't say I didn't warn you.'

'What are you thinking?'

With a reluctant sigh, she eased out of his arms and sat up, her heart aching while her head approved.

'I've got a ton of work to catch up on at the shop so I'll be leaving early in the morning.'

'Running away?'

He spoke so softly she barely caught it and couldn't read his expression in the shadows.

'We both need to get back to Melbourne.'

Back to the real world.

A world filled with monthly mortgage repayments and bills and ledgers in the red, a world far removed from hot-air balloons and late night chats over cocoa and charming billionaires hell-bent on flirting their way into her heart.

When the silence stretched between them, she blurted, 'But I'll see you at the wedding.'

'Cari invited you?'

He made it sound as if his sister would've been more likely to invite the man on the moon.

Hugging her arms around her middle, she nodded. 'You got a problem with that?'

'Do I look like I've got a problem?'

He leaned towards her, his intent clear as her heart stalled before stuttering and stomping all over the place and she shuffled backwards until her back hit the arm rest, effectively trapping her.

'If we're seeing each other at the wedding, why don't we catch up before then? There's a new hotel opening in town early next week.' He paused, almost uncertain, as he added, 'You should come with me.'

Confused, Lola searched his face for some clue as to where the invitation had come from. Was he asking her out on a date or just thought it'd be nice to catch up as friends before his sister's wedding?

She couldn't gauge much from his expression. Strangely, she could've sworn she'd seen a flicker of something when he'd asked her to the hotel opening, but it was gone so quickly she might have imagined it.

Unsure how to respond, some of her misgivings must've shown for he pinned her with an intense stare.

'As my date, in case you were wondering.'

He snagged her hand again and this time she let him, doing a happy dance on the inside.

He'd asked her out. On a date!

Instilling the right amount of casualness into her voice, she nodded. 'I'd love to.'

'Great.'

He jumped to his feet and tugged her along with him, until she was snug against his chest and his arm held her waist tight.

'Let's do a warm up dance.'

Blown away by his spontaneity, she said, 'But there's no music.'

'We'll improvise.'

With that, he held her close, leaving her no option but to rest her cheek against his chest as he hummed a hit of days gone by as they gently swayed side to side.

On a romance scale of one to ten the dance scored an eleven and as Lola's eyelids fluttered shut, she still had stars in her eyes.

Not from the view overhead but from being in the arms of the man she'd fallen for.

'You lied.'

Lola ignored Imogen, propped against the counter, as she turned and checked out her rear in the mirror, hoping this dress had been the best choice. She'd only tried on five before finally deciding.

'Lied?'

Satisfied her butt didn't look gi-normous, she leaned forward and slicked another layer of Plum Crush on her lips.

'You did do the horizontal cha-cha with Chase, otherwise you wouldn't be dressed like that.'

'I didn't!'

Not for any lack of wanting to. 'And what's wrong with the dress?'

Imogen smirked. 'Sex on legs, baby, sex on legs.'

'Rubbish.'

Though as Lola did another twirl in front of the mirror, she had to admit Imogen had a point.

The strapless magnolia satin calf-length dress embossed with violet and ebony flowers hugged her curves, the rich material draping and clinging in all the right places, making it look as if she'd been poured into it.

So what? This hotel opening was a big deal; at least, the fact Chase had asked her on a first date was a big deal and she had to look the part.

'I reckon you lied about not reading those romance novels too. That dress reeks of heroine-seducing-hot-hero material.'

Imogen rubbed her hands together. 'I want details, girlie. You've told me practically nothing since you got back from the mansion.'

'Nothing to tell,' she said, allowing herself the luxury of a small secretive smile as she remembered the kisses, the chats, the dance in the atrium.

'Your lascivious grin says otherwise.'

'You're imagining things.'

Lola quickly ducked her head on the pretext of shoving her lippie into the plum sequinned bag she'd chosen to go with the dress.

'You know, if you don't tell me anything I'll be forced to approach the source himself.' Imogen smirked. 'Oh, look, here he comes now.'

Lola's head snapped up in time to see Chase enter Go Retro and her heart danced a jig while she managed to shoot Immy a warning glare.

'Don't you dare,' she muttered under her breath as

she sashayed past Immy, working her hips to show off the dress's full potential.

That was her excuse and she was sticking to it.

'Hey Chase, I heard the hen's party went really well.'

Lola braced herself for more from her brash friend but thankfully Immy didn't push.

'Thanks to this talented woman.'

He stopped halfway across the shop, his eyes wide and fixed solely on her, the expression in those blue depths snatching her breath and making the dress feel two sizes too small.

'Wow.'

He held out his hand and she placed hers into it, allowing him to twirl her around slowly, his low wolf whistle of appreciation eliciting a laugh from Immy.

'Sexy dress, huh?'

She glared at Immy again and as Chase reeled her in, he murmured in her ear, 'Sexy woman, more like it,' creating a slow blush that started at her cleavage and worked its way upwards.

Though Imogen couldn't have heard Chase's comment, she must've got the gist from the dazed expression on his face for she made herself scarce with a blasé wave and a, 'Have a great night,' flung over her shoulder as she headed out the back.

Being alone with Chase shouldn't be this scary but the longer he stared at her with desire in those blue eyes, her fear grew exponentially.

Fear of making a fool of herself, fear of feeling too much, fear it was already too late.

'Ready to go?'

'Uh-huh.'

He held out his elbow and she threaded her arm through it, catching sight of their reflection as they headed for the door.

She'd barely said two words since he'd walked in and seeing him in a designer tux, looking better than most of the models her sister worked with, only served to tie her tongue into further knots.

He held the door open for her and she smiled her thanks. Could he be any more perfect? Another thing about the past she liked: etiquette. As far as she was concerned, old-fashioned manners should never go out of fashion.

'Lola?'

'Hmm?'

'I'm really looking forward to tonight.'

'Me too,' she murmured, lost in the heat of his gaze and knowing it was far too late to worry about falling for him further.

She'd already tumbled head first into love with him and there wasn't one darn thing she could do about it.

Chase liked being on top of things.

He liked seeing his plans come to fruition and as he watched Lola glow with excitement at something the Hotel Antiqua CEO had just said, he knew he'd made the right decision in putting her name forward for this project.

The hotel had an entire wing waiting to be decorated and what better way to go than vintage?

As Lola's hands waved around, describing some

grand plan to the CEO, he experienced a rush no other job satisfaction had come close to.

He glanced at his watch, wondering how much longer they'd have to stick around. For while the first part of his plan had gone off without a hitch, it was the second part that had him edgy.

He wanted her.

Fiercely. Uncontrollably. Relentlessly.

Every moment he stood and watched her, so vibrant, so animated, was a lesson in torture.

Tonight, he wanted to show her how much he'd enjoyed her company over the last week, wanted to make it a goodbye to remember.

Though technically he'd be seeing her at the wedding, he knew they'd be surrounded by people there and he wouldn't have a chance to tell her how truly amazing she was. Tonight, he wanted to show her.

He downed the rest of his beer, eager to leave and eternally grateful when her conversation with the CEO wound up and she looked around, trying to find him.

Taking a step forward, he raised a hand and as their gazes locked he could've sworn he felt the zap of electricity clear across the room.

Then her lips curved, a tempting plum slick in her expressive face and it took all his willpower not to shove aside the crowd separating them in his desperation to reach her.

Gliding through the crowd towards him, her eyes never left his and when the last person faded away, she flung herself into his arms with a ferocity that made his heart sing.

She hugged him fiercely and he buried his nose in her

hair, inhaling the soft fruity fragrance of her shampoo, revelling in its silkiness, reluctant to release her when she finally drew back.

'Not that I'm complaining, but what was that for?'

Her eyes burned with an inner fire he hadn't seen, vindicating the strings he'd pulled for her.

'For bringing me here.'

She jerked her head subtly to the left. 'See that guy I was talking to? He's the CEO of the hotel and we got to talking about business and what I do and he wants me to decorate an entire wing of the hotel.'

She did a funny little jig on the spot he found incredibly endearing.

'Can you believe it? It's a major job but it'll make Go Retro financially viable for years. It's a godsend, absolutely perfect timing.'

'That's great, sweetheart, congratulations.'

He hugged her, genuinely pleased. He'd never seen her so excited and the thought he'd had a hand in turning around her fortunes made him feel ten feet tall.

'Want to go celebrate?'

She tensed in his arms for a second before easing back, the flirtatious sparkle in her eyes encouraging and surprising.

'What did you have in mind?'

He crooked his finger and beckoned her forward. 'Somewhere a little more private than this.'

Trying a mock frown and failing, she said, 'Are you trying to get me alone so you can take advantage of me?'

Rubbing his hands together, he tried an evil chuckle. 'That's the plan.'

She pretended to think for a moment, before slipping her hand into his.

'What are you waiting for?'

CHAPTER TWELVE

LOLA couldn't keep the huge grin off her face.

All her problems were solved, thanks to the lucrative Hotel Antiqua contract the CEO had promised her. And she hadn't had to tender for it; he'd virtually offered it to her once they'd got chatting. She may hate asking for help but gifts like that falling into her lap? She'd grab with both hands, thank you very much.

Even now, staring out at the twinkling lights of Melbourne's skyline many storeys below, she couldn't believe that Go Retro was safe. Her blood fizzed with excitement as she mentally started planning various stages of the project from the brief tour she'd been given at the hotel.

All that space just waiting to be filled with tasteful vintage décor and furnishing, bringing a little piece of the past alive for patrons to enjoy.

The CEO had surprised her, being quite specific in what he wanted once he'd discovered what she did for a living, but she didn't question it. Why should she, when she'd been handed the opportunity of a lifetime?

Finally, *finally,* her choices had been vindicated. She'd gone out on a limb in starting Go Retro, invest- ing every cent she had, throwing herself wholeheartedly into the business despite the prophecies of doom from her folks and the usual scoffing from Shareen.

Nothing she ever did was good enough and they'd laughed at the idea of her doing anything on her own.

She'd shown them.

Without any help she'd managed to secure a lucrative contract; the publicity alone from the fit-out guaranteed to keep her in business into the next decade.

'Still basking in your glory?'

Chase came up close behind her, her skin prickling at his proximity as he handed her a wine glass.

'Can't stop thinking about it.'

'It's a great coup.'

He raised his glass and she gently clinked hers against it.

'If you hadn't taken me there I never would've met Von Deek.'

Sipping his wine, he placed the glass on a table nearby.

'Some things are meant to be.'

He wasn't talking about the chance meeting and she knew it.

Her hand trembled, the wine coming dangerously close to sloshing over the edge as he eased it out of her hand and placed the glass next to his.

She didn't know how long they stood there, tension crackling between them, their bodies straining towards each other, but the second she swayed towards him ignited a reaction she had no chance of stopping.

Their mouths clashed in a hungry kiss, his hands frantic, skimming her curves, caressing her body, eradicating any lingering doubts with his low, desperate moan.

He wanted her as much as she wanted him but the moment his hand strayed from her waist to her butt, she tensed.

Old insecurities flared: she was too big, too fat, too inexperienced, her submerged body image issues undiminished as the man she'd grown incredibly close to over the last week wanted to get naked with her.

'What's wrong?'

He eased back, his hands resting on her waist and she sighed, wishing they didn't need to have this conversation but knowing if she didn't say anything she'd end up ruining tonight anyway.

'I want this…I want us too…but…'

Tipping her chin up gently, his tender expression hit her where she feared it most: her heart.

'You're short selling yourself again, aren't you?'

Biting her bottom lip, she nodded, wondering how he did that, picking up on her emotions so easily.

'I've just never been comfortable showing my body to anyone.'

His eyes widened. 'You mean you haven't—'

'No, I've had a boyfriend.' She clamped down on the memory. 'He didn't help.'

A million questions flickered through his expressive eyes and she sighed, knowing she'd have to tell him everything.

'After I did the whole makeover thing, it took me a year to start dating. I was cautious, carefully vetting guys in case they were only using me as a stepping stone to Shareen. Bodey seemed different…'

He didn't speak, his understanding expression all the encouragement she needed to continue.

'We only dated a short time, about a month. I was pretty smitten, I thought he was too, then after we slept together...' She shrugged, not wanting to articulate how shattered she'd been after being dumped or how long she'd wondered if she'd been an experiment for him— cosy up to the chubby chick—or a challenge or, worse again, a bet.

And while Chase was nothing like Bodey, the thought of going to bed with him resurrected those old feelings of inadequacy and vulnerability, leaving her feeling raw and exposed and on edge.

'The guy's a loser.'

His harsh expletive echoed what she'd called Bodey in her mind several times over the years. 'But this isn't just about him, is it?'

She shook her head, the truth hovering on her lips. But if she told him everything, would he still want her?

'Lola?'

Going for broke, she tugged on a pinned up ringlet. 'See this?'

She pointed at her face, at the carefully applied make-up. 'And this?'

Covering his hand at her waist with hers, she smoothed it over the rich satin fabric. 'And this? All props I use to feel good about myself. I need to put on my confidence mask every day so people don't get to see the real me.'

Not backing down from a conversation that most men

would run from, he merely tightened his grip on her waist.

'The real you is a beautiful, smart, vivacious woman, the woman who snaffled my phone when we first met without blinking.'

A small smile tugged at her mouth at the memory. 'Oh, I can be bubbly and outgoing and extroverted at Go Retro because that's my comfort zone. Other times?'

She held up a hand that trembled on cue. 'I'm afraid that I use Go Retro to hide away, use it as a front for my fear of going out and taking a chance on people.'

And that was what going all the way with Chase boiled down to: taking a chance. She'd played it safe for years now, rarely dating, not socialising, burying herself in making Go Retro a success. But she knew without a shadow of a doubt if she walked away from this man now without making the most of tonight, she'd regret it every day for the rest of her life.

He opened his mouth to respond but she covered it gently with her fingertips.

'But you know something? It's times like now I realise unless I want to spend the rest of my life growing old like my merchandise, I need to step out of my comfort zone and take a chance.'

He pressed a soft kiss to her fingers before lowering them. 'Are you saying—'

'I'm terrified of you seeing the real me beneath all this fake glamour, I'm terrified of revealing my body to you and I'm really terrified of getting in any deeper than I already am, but I think it's time I took that chance.'

Standing on tiptoe, she brushed her lips against his and murmured, 'Don't you?'

Her breath hitched at the sudden flare of heat in his eyes as his gaze roved over her face, seeking reassurance and as she slowly nodded, he released her and took a step back.

Uncertain, she waited for him to say something, to do something, her body a mass of snapping synapses and zapping nerve-endings.

She inhaled sharply as he reached out and carefully pulled out one of the bobby pins holding up her curls. Then another. And another, his fingers not touching her until every last curl lay in loose disarray around her shoulders and he wound his hands through her hair, mussing it, his fingertips lightly massaging her scalp in a sigh-worthy moment bordering on erotic.

Almost boneless after a minute of the slow, sensuous scalp massage, his fingers drifted down her neck, across her collarbone and lingered on the swell of her breasts, trailing from her cleavage to the tips of her shoulders and back again, raising goose-bumps of pleasure and making her knees wobble with the intensity of her desire.

'You are truly beautiful,' he murmured, his words punctuated by the passion in his blazing stare as he slid a hand around her waist and upwards, toying with the zip on her dress.

She bit back a moan as his other hand joined the first, strumming her back with long, slow caresses, the barest of strokes eliciting a whimper when his hands moulded to her bottom and tugged her gently towards him.

'And I look forward to unveiling every glorious inch of your gorgeous body,' he whispered against the corner of her mouth before claiming it in a cataclysmic kiss that branded her as his.

A kiss that shattered any last lingering doubts, a kiss that left her mindless with wanting him, a kiss deepened to the point of no return.

There was no time for second-guessing or self-consciousness as he eased down her zip, peeling away the dress to reveal a matching corset and garter in alabaster satin, his stunned expression quickly replaced by one of awe and lust and worship.

Kneeling at her feet, his lips honed in on the smallest sliver of bare skin in the gap between her lace-top stockings and the edge of her panties, brushing against her thighs with repeated, exquisite torture.

When he finally snapped the clips on her garters she was swaying and as he rolled her silk stockings down inch by excruciating inch, she almost exploded with need.

Standing, he reached for her again. 'You—' he kissed the soft skin at the base of her throat '—are—' his fingers made deft work of the corset hooks as the satin slithered to the floor '—amazing.'

Stepping back, he cupped her breasts in his hands, his thumbs gently skimming across her nipples until she was boneless and reaching for him.

Seeing his appreciation of her body, knowing he'd taken it slow just for her, was more of an aphrodisiac than any words he could've said and, frantic to have him assuage the fire consuming her hypersensitive body, she pulled him to her and kissed him, crushing her breasts against his chest, her pelvis arching towards him.

She couldn't stop wanting this man any more than she

could give up her dream and with her desire clamouring for release, she matched him stride for stride as he backed her towards the bedroom.

Where with his skilful hands and mouth and body, he revelled in her body and made her feel truly beautiful for the first time ever.

Lola lay awake in the darkness, clutching the sheet to her breasts, realising how foolish she was being yet unable to shake the feeling that Chase would wake any moment and regret what they'd done.

Repeatedly.

Over the last few hours.

Besides, too late for modesty now. He'd seen all of her, had caressed every inch of her body and come back for seconds and the memory alone made her skin flush.

Thankfully, he hadn't made a big deal out of her insistence he turn the light off. She'd phrased her request persuasively, implying it would heighten their pleasure if they relied on touch.

And touch her he did, making her cry out his name, making her desperate for him, making her want this night to never end. Yet the minute he'd drifted into deep slumber the insecurities had started. Had she made a mistake in sleeping with him? Would he move on now to the next challenge?

For she was under no illusions that was why he seemed so fascinated by her: she was different to the women he usually mixed with.

She had no expectations of him, wasn't overly impressed by his wealth or status and realistically saw no future for them.

Liar.

Chase stirred and her grip on the sheet tightened. Okay, so maybe she had envisioned a happily-ever-after scenario for them. She wouldn't be here otherwise, more vulnerable than ever, her body and heart exposed.

And the longer she lay here in his bed, mentally re-hashing every romantic moment they'd spent together her imagination had her one step further up the aisle.

For that was what she ultimately wanted: a husband, a house, a posse of kids and the freedom to be who she wanted to be and loved for it.

Her love of vintage incorporated a reverence for old-fashioned values and she was kidding herself if she hadn't seen Chase in the role of adoring husband. She may be a modern girl but there was nothing wrong with home-cooked meals and a cosy house and a family to fill it with love and warmth and appreciation for one another.

Things she hadn't grown up with. By the sounds of it Chase hadn't grown up with them either but did that mean he craved it like she did or would he run from that whole scene?

Considering his single status and playboy reputation, she had a strong suspicion it was the latter.

He stirred again and she stiffened, holding her breath when his hand casually draped over her stomach and splayed on her hip.

She'd planned on easing out of bed and hiding out in the bathroom to get dressed before he woke but as his grip tightened and his eyelids cranked open, she knew the time for making a graceful escape had passed.

'Hey, come here, you.'

He tugged her closer, brushing a soft, lingering kiss across her lips, his eyes hazy with sleep and satisfaction.

'Some night, huh?'

All she could manage was a mumbled, 'Uh-huh,' her heart instantly kicking into second gear at the sight of those blue eyes locking onto her.

'I knew getting the hotel contract would show you how much I've enjoyed our time together. Last night was amazing.'

He shifted towards her but she placed a hand against his chest, her mind still processing what he'd just said. Something about the hotel contract…and as she stared at him in dawning horror all he could do was smile with pride, as if he'd bestowed the greatest gift on her.

'*You* arranged for me to get that contract?'

To her relief, her voice didn't quiver while inside she screamed at having her success belittled and ripped apart before she'd had a proper chance to savour it.

His expression sheepish, he shrugged. 'We've had a great time together and nothing I said was getting through so I thought I'd pull a few strings—'

'I can't believe you did that.'

Shaking her head, she frantically tugged at the top sheet, sliding out of bed in an ungraceful heap before wrapping it around her.

'Do you know what it meant to me, knowing I did that on my own? Achieving something? Proving all the sceptics wrong? Do you?'

Her voice had risen and she clamped her lips shut, hating the hint of hysteria.

Frowning, he sat up and thankfully pulled the duvet over his lower half.

'By your over the top reaction, I'm beginning to see.'

'Over the top?'

She gritted her teeth against the urge to fling something at him. How could he not understand? He worked hard, he was successful—surely he'd know what this meant to her?

But as he sat there on the edge of the crumpled bed, confusion slowly replaced by anger at her outburst, she realised something she'd known all along.

He couldn't understand because they were too different. And all the kisses and cosy chats and snuggles in the world wouldn't change that.

'I'm leaving.'

'You're overreacting,' he said, reaching for her but she evaded him as she managed an unladylike squat to scoop up her dress and underwear from the floor.

With a poise she'd acquired through years of practice, she stopped at the bedroom door and pinned him with a haughty stare.

'For you to say that just shows you don't know me at all.'

Hating it had come to this, she held up an underwear-filled hand, inwardly grimacing with embarrassment.

'If you value anything that has happened between us, please let me leave.'

'Lola, this is nuts—'

'Goodbye, Chase.'

She slammed the bedroom door for extra emphasis, grateful the loud sound masked her first sob.

Chase waited until he heard the front door closing before swinging his legs out of bed and sitting up.

Every stunned cell in his body wanted to go running after Lola, to call her back, to talk sense into her.

She'd overreacted, taken his goodwill gesture as interfering and that really peed him off. How many times had he gone the extra yard as a kid, putting extra effort into his studies and his sports, hoping his folks would understand how much their opinion mattered?

When most of his mates had been hanging around at the local skate ramp having a good time he'd been looking after Cari, playing housekeeper and chef, wishing the people who mattered most would appreciate his gestures.

His parents never had. The only time they'd come close to acknowledging his efforts was when they'd given him their precious armoire when he'd graduated from high school, the first piece of furniture they'd bought when they'd got married.

He'd thought it had meant a lot until they'd belittled it with a, 'If you have this, you might study something useful rather than play around with figures and chase money.'

He'd kept it anyway, letting it take pride of place in his lounge as a reminder to never make the mistake of trusting his heart. Though after a busy week, as he sat in his lounge sipping a whisky, he'd stare at that blasted armoire and knew that deep down it represented something else entirely—a time when his parents had noticed him, one of the good times, a time he'd give anything to have again.

The only reason why he still visited his folks despite the past was because he cared. Just like he cared about Lola. Doing something for people he cared about only to have his good intentions ripped to shreds hurt like the devil and having the woman he loved react the same way his folks did most times had him leaping off the bed and pacing the bedroom, fists clenched, inhaling huge lungfuls of air to calm the urge to vent.

It must've been on his third circuit when he realised what he'd just thought.

The woman he loved...

Hell.

Since when had this moved beyond having fun?

A plethora of flashbacks flitted across his mind: Lola curled up on the couch in his study cradling her cocoa, Lola's wondrous expression as the hot-air balloon lifted off, Lola warm and lush in his arms as they danced in the atrium's moonlight, Lola's sparkling eyes every time they kissed.

Each snippet of memory, every tantalising flashback, coalesced into a giant whole, tightening his chest, squeezing his heart until he rubbed the spot over it.

He'd never fallen in love before. Why now? With a woman who so obviously didn't understand him it was painful.

At the office, when a deal went south he'd sit down and make a list of pros and cons, then do everything in his power to make the pros work in his favour.

Considering the way Lola had stormed out of here, he had a feeling no amount of list-making would help.

Swiping a hand over his face, he padded towards the bathroom. A shower might clear his head, help clarify what he needed to do.

Right now, that entailed figuring out what the hell he was going to do with this alien feeling invading his cool business brain and making him want to do crazy things.

Like find Lola as soon as possible and grovel.

Lola cringed every time she checked her mobile phone for messages.

It was the end of the week; surely if Chase wanted to get in touch he would've done it by now?

Not that she expected him to, not after the way she'd behaved, but a small part of her, the part that loved him, wished he felt one iota of genuine emotion in return, an emotion that might prompt him to ring the crazy woman who'd shattered her own dreams in one neurotic outburst.

Her behaviour had bordered on neurotic and she deliberately wiped the memory of that night every time it surfaced—which was often, thanks to what had come before her little meltdown.

She'd never known making love could be like that. Bodey may have awakened her sexuality six years ago but compared to Chase, he was a beginner.

Her body had sung beneath Chase's expert hands… and mouth… In shedding her clothes for Chase she'd opened herself up in a way she'd never thought possible again and for those brief few hours when he'd caressed and stroked and cherished, her size hadn't mattered for the first time.

She loved him, she knew that, otherwise she never would've put herself in that situation. But all the whispered words of endearment and all the soul-drugging kisses in the world couldn't totally eradicate the same insecure girl she'd always been.

Then learning he'd been the one behind her biggest business coup after she'd laid her heart open like that... Well, all those old feelings had built to the point where she could see nothing but a guy who thrived on control, a guy who wanted to mould her a certain way to fit into his world, a guy who could never accept her for who she really was: an old-fashioned girl who'd love nothing better than to settle down with the right guy, indulge her passion for food and build a real home with him.

Sadly, she knew Chase couldn't be that man. She'd always known it but had allowed her yearning for him to blind her, desperate to take what she could get before her prince vanished into the wide blue yonder with another stick-figure-It-girl.

Now she had to face him at Cari's wedding, a fact that made her palms clammy as she sorted inventory. She'd thought about calling him, trying to smooth things over before the wedding, but her throat seized up every time.

Besides, it wasn't as if she'd make a scene or anything. It was Cari's big day and she'd be the epitome of polite when she ran into him. Or with a bit of luck, he'd waltz into the wedding with some knockout blonde a hundred times sexier than her and that would be the end of that.

Don't undersell yourself.

She stopped dead, the scarves in her hands sliding

to the floor as the echo of Chase's words taunted her, making a mockery of her previous thought.

It wouldn't be lucky if Chase brought a beautiful date to the wedding. She'd *hate* it. Just like she hated how things had ended between them.

She could take the easy way out and hide among the mannequins here or she could resurrect some of her chutzpah from the other night and take another chance. Show up at Cari's wedding. In a killer dress. With a sturdy resolve to make things right.

Decision made, she nodded at a mannequin draped in a crushed cerise velvet cloak that stared balefully back at her and scooped up the fallen scarves. The sooner she finished running inventory the sooner she could make a start on finding that killer dress.

Weddings always made Lola cry and Cari's was no exception.

She sniffed as Cari strolled along the flower-strewn red carpet towards her groom standing under a towering eucalypt.

She dabbed her eyes as the happy couple exchanged vows.

And she scrabbled madly in her bag for another tissue or ten when they kissed and Hugh swung his bride around in a bear hug until she squealed.

Being utterly absorbed in watching Cari and Hugh might have turned on the waterworks but it served another purpose: to avoid locking gazes with Chase at all costs.

They'd managed to exchange stiff pleasantries when she'd first arrived but thankfully she'd been swallowed into the festivities at the insistence of the four Bs, resplendent in flowing silk gowns of varying pastel shades, flitting around like ethereal butterflies.

Yet she knew the time for avoidance was over as the couple made their way to the atrium for pre-dinner drinks, most of the guests following.

All but one.

As Chase strode towards her, incredibly sexy in his designer tux, she had the urge to bolt, to run like she'd always done from confrontation. She'd never stood up for herself as a kid, had been ordered around by a mother expecting perfection and a sister who liked being bossy for the heck of it.

She'd slunk in their shadows, resentful yet powerless to do anything about it. Until she'd finally grown a spine and moved to Melbourne and come into her own. She was proud of the person she'd become, the type of person who could attract the interest of a guy like Chase. But after the way she'd behaved, could she keep it?

Her heart stalled as he stopped in front of her, a flicker of uncertainty in his eyes quickly masked by his usual savoir faire.

'It's great to see you,' he said, brushing a kiss across her cheek as if it was the most natural thing in the world.

Resisting the urge to cup her cheek and hold onto that kiss for ever, she managed a smile. 'The wedding was gorgeous.'

'Cari's happy, that's the main thing.'

The warmth in his eyes faded as he glanced to an older couple hovering uncertainly by the gazebo.

'No thanks to them.'

The couple, dressed surprisingly casually in matching khaki slacks and button-down white shirts, held hands tightly, as if afraid to let each other go and get swept away in the party atmosphere. They looked out of place, uncomfortable, as if a beautiful dusk wedding in the Mount Macedon ranges was the last place they'd want to be.

'Your folks?'

'Uh-huh.'

So much bitterness in those two tiny syllables and before she could think she reached out and clasped his hand and squeezed.

'Hey, at least they made it.'

A hundred different emotions flashed across his face before he tore his gaze from them and focused on her, his uncertainty surprising her as much as the vulnerability.

'Yeah. It meant a lot to Cari, having them here, I could tell.'

She squeezed his hand, trying to convey understanding and sympathy. 'You did good, getting them here.'

The tightness around his mouth eased. 'I did it for Cari.'

'I think they came for you too.'

Confusion creased his brow as she released his hand and tried a subtle thumb jerk in the direction of his parents. 'Incoming.'

'What—'

Putting on her best Go Retro face, Lola held out her hand. 'Hi, I'm Lola, a friend of Chase and Cari's.'

Chase's mum shook her hand in a surprisingly

firm grip. 'Belinda Etheridge. And this is my husband Bert.'

His dad nodded. 'Pleased to meet you.'

An awkward silence reigned for a split second before Chase said, 'Glad you came.'

'We wouldn't have missed it.' To her surprise, and Chase's too by the way his eyebrows shot up, Belinda squeezed his arm. 'Some things are just more important than academia.'

'Pity it's taken us thirty years to realise it,' Bert mumbled and by the stunned expression on Chase's face, his shock was complete.

Lola wished she could extricate herself gracefully from this long overdue family heart to heart but the moment she sidled away an inch, Chase's hand shot out and grabbed hers.

'Drinks are being served in the atrium.' He cleared his throat, his vulnerability making her heart ache. 'Maybe if you have time later, we can catch up?'

'We'd love that.' Belinda quickly kissed his cheek, as if expecting a rebuff and Bert clapped him on the back. 'You've got a fine place here, son. You've done well for yourself.' Almost as an afterthought, he added, 'We're proud of you.'

Since Lola had met Chase he'd never been speechless. Today was a first as they watched his parents meander their way towards the house.

'Pinch me.'

Lola smiled. 'You're not dreaming.'

Releasing her hand, he rubbed the back of his neck, his wistful gaze focused on his parents' retreating backs. 'I can't believe that just happened. I mean, it's good enough having them here for Cari but all that stuff they said…' He cleared his throat again and she yearned to hug him. 'I've been waiting a lifetime to hear it.'

'I'm so happy for you.'

'Catching up later will be interesting to say the least.' He shook his head, as if trying to clear his daze. 'There's so much we need to catch up on…'

'It's great you never gave up on them.'

'You've probably done the same.'

His assessing stare made her squirm, as she realised he was right. Despite her upbringing, she still loved her folks and Shareen, still wanted their approval. Though lately, that hadn't mattered so much… It struck her then how since she'd met Chase and he'd lavished attention on her, she hadn't felt the need for approval.

She was more confident in herself, more sure of her assets than she'd ever been. Having the approval of people who'd criticised her growing up wasn't so important now she was successful in her own right, and having confidence in her body grew exponentially with the adulation of the right man.

Chase was that man.

'Yeah, I guess you're right. I don't give up on people.'

'That's one of the things I admire about you—your faith in people. Your ability to see the best in them, to bring out the best in others.'

He tightened his grip on her hand. 'Thanks to you, I'm seeing people in a new light too.'

Not sure where he was heading with this, she gave him an encouraging smile.

'What I'm trying to say is, I used to be caught up in the entertainment industry twenty-four-seven. I worked it, I partied with it. I went from one shallow date to the next, not really caring about anyone bar Cari.'

His thumb brushed the back of her hand and her resolve to see him at the wedding and say a proper good-bye shook to its foundations.

'Then I met you. You're warm, vibrant, genuinely beautiful inside and out, and you made me want to share in that warmth too.'

He waved his free hand around the property. 'I rarely came out here but having you here made me see that a home isn't about sleek lines and modern furniture, it's about creating a place filled with cooking and laughter and moonlit dances.'

A huge lump welled in her throat. She couldn't have answered him if she'd wanted to.

'Thanks to you, I'm going to head out here more often. I'm going to take time out to chill rather than running on a city treadmill all day every day.'

Reaching out to pluck a rose, he waved it beneath her nose until she laughed. 'I'm going to take time out to smell these.'

Uncharacteristically bashful, he handed her the rose. 'I'm really glad you showed up today. I thought you should know all that stuff.'

'I wouldn't miss it. Cari invited me, I had to come.'

'For Cari.'

The wariness was back in his voice, tingeing his tone with uncertainty.

Taking a deep breath, she tilted her head up. 'For me too.'

He didn't answer, giving her the floor to deliver what promised to be one heck of a speech.

'It's taken me the week to build up the courage to see you again.'

His eyebrows shot up. 'You're scared to face me?'

She winced. 'Embarrassed more like it.'

Shaking her head, she said, 'I overreacted that night... when we...'

He wasn't making this easy on her and she ploughed straight in.

'This may sound crazy but I spent most of my life being controlled by my mum, trying to live up to her expectations. She organised what I'd wear, what I'd eat, where I'd go, who I'd socialise with. My whole life revolved around Shareen and Mum made damn sure I was along for the ride.'

Swallowing the lump of emotion that always arose when she strolled down memory lane, she continued.

'My opinions didn't matter. What I liked didn't matter. I soon learned it was easier to go along with everything than make waves so I did.'

She found herself tugging absentmindedly on a curl and tucked it firmly behind her ear.

'When I came to Melbourne I vowed to never be controlled by anyone again.'

'But I wasn't—'

'Let me finish.' She held up her hand. 'Being in control has meant shutting myself off from people, men especially, emotionally.'

Ignoring her churning belly, she went for broke. 'You're the first guy in years I've got close to and opening myself up to you in every way made me go a little nuts.'

'You thought I'd hurt you.' Shrewd as ever, his eyes narrowed. 'Like that creep?'

She didn't think he was anything like Bodey, not any more, but she'd started this, she had to finish it.

'Guess I was wary. Once I slept with him he wasn't interested in the fat chick any more.'

Fury flushed his face, his arms shooting out to grab her before she could move.

'I'm nothing like that jerk. I—we—ah, hell.'

He released her and jammed a hand through his hair, the first time she'd seen anything other than slick and styled.

He paced a few steps before swinging back to her, his expression wild-eyed.

'I'm in love with you,' he blurted, looking anything but pleased by the declaration that had her grabbing a nearby tree for support.

'This isn't how I planned on telling you but I've missed you so much and I had this list of pros and cons I made and I wanted to ring you or turn up at your shop but the longer I left it the harder it got and—'

'Shh…'

She placed her fingers over his lips. 'Let's take a step back to that loving part.'

With a goofy grin that made her heart flip, he snagged both her hands in his.

'Honestly? I don't know what love is. I date, I don't do love. But this crazy, unstoppable, clamouring feeling for you invading my thoughts twenty-four-seven must be love because I know right now I can't live another moment without you.'

Oh-oh, there went her tear ducts again, as tears of joy trickled down her face.

Sheer terror streaked across his face before her wobbly smile allayed his fears.

'That's the nicest thing anyone's ever said to me.'

Tugging on her hands, he hauled her into his arms and hugged tight until she could barely breathe.

'Get used to it, sweetheart. There's a lifetime more where that came from.'

Light-headed from lack of oxygen, she eased back and looked into the eyes of the man she loved.

'Are you saying—'

'I'm saying I want to grow old with you, right alongside all that fluff and frippery you're into so much.'

Before she could say she loved him right back and would like nothing better than to spend a lifetime in his arms, he swooped, his mouth crushing hers in a breath-stealing, toe-curling, resistance-shattering kiss that had her laughing and sniffling and clinging to him all at the same time.

'So what do you say?'

She wanted to say yes. She wanted to scream it with all the air in her lungs that this amazing, gorgeous, sexy man wanted her.

But a lifetime of insecurity gnawed at her newfound happiness, refusing to be ignored.

'We're so different.'

His smile faded, his eyes clouding with confusion. 'That's your answer?'

He released her and she instantly craved the strength of his arms again. Looking like she'd just struck him, he shook his head.

'I lay my heart on the line, I give it to you straight, and you say we're too different?'

Way out of her depth, she floundered for a response to make him understand how totally flummoxed she was.

'Chase, let me explain—'

'Of course we're different. I knew that the moment I walked into your shop.'

She saw the silent plea in those heart-stopping blue eyes and it tore her apart.

'But that's not why I want to be with you. I couldn't care less if you wore your hair curled every day or came to bed wearing a boned corset.'

She blushed but he continued, oblivious. 'All this?' He waved at her outfit, her hair. 'Irrelevant, because it's you I love. The real you. Inside here.'

His hand hovered over her heart and she held her breath, wishing he'd touch her, terrified he would.

'If a guy who had no clue how to love before this is willing to take a chance, why can't you?'

Good question, but she didn't want to answer, didn't want to tell him her deepest fears, her deepest regrets. For if she truly opened up to him, would he still want her?

Yet if she didn't, she'd lose him anyway.

'Lola, I'm dying here.'

Reluctantly raising her eyes to his, she blurted, 'What if I'm not good enough for you?'

His jaw dropped. 'What the—'

'I know it's crazy to feel this way but most of my life I didn't live up to expectations. Too fat, too ugly, too quiet, too mousy.'

He opened his mouth to protest again and she held up a hand.

'It's lame blaming this on my mum and my sister because I should've stood up for myself a long time ago, but when I finally did I may've changed how I look on the outside but it didn't really change how I felt inside.'

'But you're gorgeous! And confident.'

His mouth quirked into a smile. 'No other woman has ever had the audacity to separate me from my smart-phone and you did it within seconds of meeting me.'

She smiled at the memory. 'Being in Go Retro, surrounded by my dream always gives me a boost. Most of the time, though…' she screwed up her nose '…I'm the same insecure little mouse inside just craving approval.'

Understanding lit his eyes and she sighed in relief.

'So why do you think you wouldn't be good enough for me?'

'Look at you, for goodness' sake! Look at this place!' She waved her hand towards the house, the grounds.

'We're worlds apart. I'm nothing like you. I'm old-fashioned, you're addicted to your mod cons. You're an A-lister, I'm lucky to make a Z list. You're sociable, I prefer staying home. And once the novelty of my differences wears off, what's to say—'

He kissed her again, effectively silencing the rest of her arguments and making her forget what most of them were in the first place.

All sense of time and place faded under the skilled onslaught of his lips and as she clung to him, every logical reason they shouldn't do this evaporated into the dusk.

When his lips finally eased, he rested his forehead on hers.

'Everything I do, everything I've ever done, I do for keeps. Even my folks, who've done their best to show they don't give a damn about me, I've stuck by, because that's the type of guy I am.'

Lifting his head, he stared straight into her eyes. 'I'm a long haul guy. In this for ever. So I'm going to ask you one more time. What do you say?'

She stared at his face, into his eyes, searching for the slightest flicker of doubt, of deception, of disengenuousness, and found none.

A solid, true, genuine love blazed from those eyes she'd fallen for practically the first moment she'd seen them and, in that instant, she knew what her answer had to be.

'I say you're the most amazing, gorgeous, charming man and I love you to bits. I say yes!'

She laughed as his arms clamped around her waist and spun her around until she was dizzy. When they finally stopped, she slid down, her body mesmerisingly plastered to his, the instant heat between them warming her cheeks.

'Though there is just one more thing...'

Not letting her go, he nuzzled her neck. 'Whatever it is, we'll deal with it.'

'My real name's not Lola.'

His head snapped up. 'Huh?'

Blushing, she screwed up her nose. 'I hated being boring old Louise being bossed around her whole life so when I came to Melbourne and reinvented myself, I changed my name by deed poll to Lola. Think I'm mad?'

With a relieved chuckle, he shook his head. 'I think you're wonderful, whatever you're called.'

Trailing a fingertip down his cheek, she traced his lips, stunned and thrilled she'd get to do this for the rest of her life.

'You know I love you to the heavens and back, right?'

With a slow, sexy smile that made her melt, he jerked his head towards the house.

'Once the reception is over, you can show me exactly how much.'

With racing hearts, they headed for the house, ready for one hell of a party.

And eager to get to the real celebration later, much later.

EPILOGUE

THE party of the year was in full swing at Melbourne's newest hot spot, the Hotel Antiqua, when the guests of honour arrived.

Cameras flashed, patrons oohed and ahhed, and reporters for newspaper society columns scribbled furiously in their notebooks as Lola Lombard entered the ballroom she'd designed on the arm of her fiancé, mega-successful entertainment guru Chase Etheridge.

People gasped at her dress, a strapless bodice embroidered with crystals and ice-blue chiffon handkerchief layers cascading to the floor, her hair, soft golden ringlets piled high on her head and anchored with a diamanté bow and her shoes, towering silver stilettos adorned with shoe buckles matching the bow in her hair, while her adoring fiancé looked on, delighted to bask in the limelight of his successful wife-to-be.

Everyone wanted a piece of the glamour couple and it wasn't till a full hour had passed did they finally slip away.

Chase led Lola to the rooftop, pushing open the door and gesturing her ahead of him.

'You know your impeccable manners were one of the many things that impressed me when we first met?'

He patted her bottom as she squeezed past. 'That and my sizeable—'

'Ego,' she finished, blushing.

'I was going to say mansion.'

He winked and her heart expanded until she thought it'd burst.

How had she got so lucky? A thriving business, a new close friend in Cari who she caught up with weekly, and the man of her dreams.

A man who'd cut back on his manic work hours so they could spend weekends at Mount Macedon, a man who encouraged and supported her, a man who made her laugh, a man who adored her.

She'd never felt so cherished, so appreciated, so loved, and she thanked her lucky stars every day she'd taken a chance and let him into her life, her heart.

'So what's up here…? Oh…'

She gaped as Chase led her out onto the rooftop. She'd expected flat concrete with a killer view. Instead, the rooftop had been transformed into a garden, lush with ferns and palms edging a gazebo, with freesias and frangipanis spilling out of giant terracotta pots.

'It's gorgeous.'

'There's more.' Smiling, he tilted her chin up. 'Take a look overhead.'

A million stars twinkled overhead, soft moonlight washing everything in an incandescent glow and she breathed out a reverent sigh. 'This reminds me of that night in your atrium.'

'When we danced to no music?'

He slid an arm around her waist, took hold of her hand. 'Like this?'

They swayed side to side, their bodies fitting perfectly, her curves to his hardness, lost in a world where love was the only music required.

An exquisite eternity later, he eased away, cupping her face between his hands and kissing her.

'I love you.'

Smiling against his mouth, she whispered, 'Right back at you,' before slanting her lips across his, wishing they could stay up here for ever.

However, Chase had other ideas as he released her and snagged her hand. 'Come on.'

'Where are you taking me?'

He wiggled a finger at her and held onto her hand more tightly. 'It's a surprise.'

'Out here?'

'Trust me, you'll love it.'

He led her down the stairs and into a private ballroom where Chase's family and hers stood around what suspiciously looked like a minister. She stumbled and would've fallen if her steadfast fiancé hadn't gripped her hand.

Clutching onto him, she halted just inside the doorway, stunned to see her folks and Shareen, even more shocked to see them smiling at her with pride.

'What...when...how...why...?'

He laughed and swept her into his arms, lowering his head to murmur in her ear, 'You said you didn't want a big fancy wedding so I thought we'd do a small, intimate family affair right here. The how? Well, you know I'm an ingenious businessman so I made a few phone calls, pulled a few strings and got the gang together.'

'Some gang,' she muttered, still in shock at seeing

her supermodel sister deigning to be here let alone make polite small talk with Chase's folks, who'd actually been making more of an effort with their son since Cari's wedding.

'As for the why... Well, I would've thought that's obvious.'

He pressed a hot, lingering kiss just beneath her ear and she bit back a moan as the familiar fire raced through her body at his touch.

'We're really getting married?'

Laughing, he picked her up and swung her around as their audience applauded.

'We really, really are.'

With her heart swelling with so much love for this amazing man she thought it'd burst, she gently pummelled his shoulders until he put her down.

'Come on then, what are we waiting for?'

Harlequin® Romance

Coming Next Month

Available August 9, 2011

#4255 LITTLE COWGIRL NEEDS A MOM
Patricia Thayer
The Quilt Shop in Kerry Springs

#4256 TO WED A RANCHER
Myrna Mackenzie

#4257 THE SECRET PRINCESS
Jessica Hart
The Princess Swap

#4258 MR. RIGHT THERE ALL ALONG
Jackie Braun
The Fun Factor

#4259 A KISS TO SEAL THE DEAL
Nikki Logan

#4260 THE ARMY RANGER'S RETURN
Soraya Lane
Heroes Come Home

You can find more information on upcoming
Harlequin® titles, free excerpts and more at
www.HarlequinInsideRomance.com.

HRCNM0711

Once bitten, twice shy. That's Gabby Wade's motto—
especially when it comes to Adamson men.
And the moment she meets Jon Adamson her theory
is confirmed. But with each encounter a little something
sparks between them, making her wonder if she's been
too hasty to dismiss this one!

Enjoy this sneak peek from ONE GOOD REASON
by Sarah Mayberry, available August 2011
from Harlequin® Superromance®.

Gabby Wade's heartbeat thumped in her ears as she marched to her office. She wanted to pretend it was because of her brisk pace returning from the file room, but she wasn't that good a liar.

Her heart was beating like a tom-tom because Jon Adamson had touched her. In a very male, very possessive way. She could still feel the heat of his big hand burning through the seat of her khakis as he'd steadied her on the ladder.

It had taken every ounce of self-control to tell him to unhand her. What she'd really wanted was to grab him by his shirt and, well, explore all those urges his touch had instantly brought to life.

While she might not like him, she was wise enough to understand that it wasn't always about liking the other person. Sometimes it was about pure animal attraction.

Refusing to think about it, she turned to work. When she'd typed in the wrong figures three times, Gabby admitted she was too tired and too distracted. Time to call it a day.

As she was leaving, she spied Jon at his workbench in the shop. His head was propped on his hand as he studied blueprints. It wasn't until she got closer that she saw his eyes were shut.

He looked oddly boyish. There was something innocent and unguarded in his expression. She felt a weakening in her resistance to him.

"Jon." She put her hand on his shoulder, intending to shake him awake. Instead, it rested there like a caress.

His eyes snapped open.

"You were asleep."

"No, I was, uh, visualizing something on this design." He gestured to the blueprint in front of him then rubbed his eyes.

That gesture dealt a bigger blow to her resistance. She realized it wasn't only animal attraction pulling them together. She took a step backward as if to get away from the knowledge.

She cleared her throat. "I'm heading off now."

He gave her a smile, and she could see his exhaustion.

"Yeah, I should, too." He stood and stretched. The hem of his T-shirt rose as he arched his back and she caught a flash of hard male belly. She looked away, but it was too late. Her mind had committed the image to permanent memory.

And suddenly she knew, for good or bad, she'd never look at Jon the same way again.

Find out what happens next in ONE GOOD REASON, available August 2011 from Harlequin® Superromance®!

Celebrating

Blaze **10** *years of*
red-hot reads

Featuring a special August author lineup of
six fan-favorite authors who have written
for Blaze™ from the beginning!

The Original Sexy Six:

Vicki Lewis Thompson
Tori Carrington
Kimberly Raye
Debbi Rawlins
Julie Leto
Jo Leigh

Pick up all six Blaze™
Special Collectors' Edition titles!

August 2011

Plus visit
HarlequinInsideRomance.com
and click on the Series Excitement Tab
for exclusive Blaze™ 10th Anniversary content!

www.Harlequin.com

SPECIAL EDITION

Life, Love, Family and Top Authors!

IN AUGUST, HARLEQUIN SPECIAL EDITION FEATURES
USA TODAY BESTSELLING AUTHORS
MARIE FERRARELLA AND *ALLISON LEIGH.*

THE BABY WORE A BADGE
BY *MARIE FERRARELLA*

The second title in the **Montana Mavericks:
The Texans Are Coming!** miniseries....

Suddenly single father Jake Castro has his hands full with
the baby he never expected—and with a beautiful young
woman too wise for her years.

COURTNEY'S BABY PLAN
BY *ALLISON LEIGH*

The third title in the **Return to the Double C** miniseries....

Tired of waiting for Mr. Right, nurse Courtney Clay takes
matters into her own hands to create the family she's
always wanted— but her surly patient may just be
the Mr. Right she's been searching for all along.

**Look for these titles and others in August 2011
from Harlequin Special Edition wherever books are sold.**

BIG SKY BRIDE, BE MINE! *(Northridge Nuptials)* by *VICTORIA PADE*
THE MOMMY MIRACLE by *LILIAN DARCY*
THE MOGUL'S MAYBE MARRIAGE by *MINDY KLASKY*
LIAM'S PERFECT WOMAN by *BETH KERY*

---

www.Harlequin.com

SEUSA0811